COUNTRY ROMANCE

CAROLYNE AARSEN

CHAPTER ONE

"I guess this is the ranch." Adele checked the map on her phone. The blue flashing dot showing her current location was right on the coordinates she received in Millars Crossing.

She turned to look at her passenger in the back seat of her car.

Dean was fast asleep, his head cocked at an awkward angle, his chubby cheeks rosy red, his down-filled jacket open.

The five-year-old boy was exhausted, and Adele didn't blame him. Today they had driven for six hours. Eight hours the day before and seven previous to that.

Now they had arrived at their destination and her stomach clenched with nerves. Adele looked down the winding road leading to the cluster of buildings nestled against the rolling hills and back-dropped by the mountains in the distance. The hills were still blanketed with snow sparkling in the deceptive sunshine. The temperature gauge on her car showed that it was still icily cold outside, and a sudden gust of wind tossed snow from the freshly plowed ditch over the road.

If she was a praying person, like her foster mother had been, Adele would have been sending up many of them now. She wasn't looking forward to the trip down to the ranch or relaying the news she was about to drop into Wyatt Sutton's life.

Wyatt, the owner of the ranch spread out below her, had never met Dean. Had never even heard of him.

He had no clue Dean was his son, and she wondered if Wyatt even knew her friend Sally had been his mother.

Though Sally and her ex-husband hadn't been married long, Adele always assumed that he was Dean's father, and Sally had never told her different.

Then Sally was diagnosed with a fast-growing and inoperable stomach cancer. As she lay dying, she told Adele the truth. That Dean was Wyatt Sutton's child. That she hadn't told Wyatt, because after Dean was born, she found out Wyatt had gotten married. So, she had kept it secret all this time.

But now she was dying. Her parents were gone, and Sally had no other family. She wanted Adele to bring Dean to his biological father, the only living relative Dean had.

Adele hoped his wife would be understanding.

The plan had seemed straightforward. Show this Wyatt person Dean's birth certificate, remind Wyatt of his and Sally's brief relationship and his responsibility toward his son.

Hope and pray that Wyatt's wife would forgive him.

Now that Adele was looking at the buildings where the gas-station owner in the town of Millars Crossing had told her Wyatt Sutton lived, the amorphous plan became scarily real.

All the long drive from Whitehorse Adele was still dealing with the grief of losing her friend. Was busy trying to keep Dean happy. Planning where they would stay in the next town they were headed towards.

Now they had come to the end of the road.

Adele had booked an Airbnb in Millars Crossing but hadn't gone there, preferring to get the hardest part of her trip behind her.

She wished she could have called ahead, but she had no information on Wyatt Sutton. Only the town where he lived in thanks to the magic of Google and the directions she got in town.

"Okay, buddy, here we go," Adele said, sucking in a deep, calming breath. She put the car in gear, hoping the ancient tires on her vehicle would keep her on the winding, snow-covered road leading to the ranch. The car slithered and slid a few times, so with her heart in her throat she slowed to a crawl, trying to keep her focus on the road and not on the amazing view opening up in front of her.

Her nerves were jangling by the time she pulled up beside a black pickup parked in front of a large log house nestled against a copse of spruce and pine. Floor-to-ceiling windows on one side of the house overlooked a frozen pond. A large wrap-around porch held metal chairs and a table, all covered with snow.

Past the house she saw a hip-roof barn with corrals connected to it. A few horses stared over the wooden fence at her, as if wondering what she was doing here. Beyond the barn was a large metal shed housing farming equipment and, beside that, what looked like a shop with a huge overhead door. A few more outbuildings were scattered beyond that. What looked like an older house and a smaller cabin beside that.

She pulled in another breath, hoping this would go better than her imaginings.

He's a good man, Sally had assured her.

That may be, but Adele just hoped he had married a good woman. An understanding woman.

Adele zipped up her down coat, pulled the hood up, tugged on her mittens, and stepped out of the car into the frigid air.

Shivering, she walked around the car and opened the back passenger door.

Dean lifted his head and smiled at her.

The sight twisted her stomach. Dean was only three when he and Sally moved in with Adele. He'd been a part of her life for two years. How could she just drop him off?

Because you're not his mother and he needs to be with his father. Family stays with family. Family stays together.

And her other reality was, she couldn't take care of Dean on her own. She and Sally managed because they worked different shifts, so Dean spent minimal time in day care. They had pooled their money for expenses. They shared the rent.

There was no way Adele could do this on her own. Not while trying to save money for the dream bakery she had planned for ever since her foster mother first taught her how to make cookies.

Adele knew firsthand what it was like to have no roots. She'd bounced between her foster home and her father's home too much in her life. Dean needed the stability Adele couldn't give him.

Then there was the whole faith issue.

Sally had been raised in a strong Christian home and, despite her momentary lapses, still taught Dean about God and Jesus.

One more thing Adele couldn't give Dean.

Dean stretched his arms over his head then yawned, shivering as the cold winter air seeped into the car.

"Do we need to put gas in the car?" he asked, blinking as he sat up and looked around, confused.

"No. We're finally here. At the ranch."

Dean gave her a huge smile that tore at Adele's heart. All the way here he'd talked about how fun it would be to have a dad. How excited he was to live on a ranch. Though he was still grieving his mother's death, what had kept him going was the

4

stories his mother had spun about how much fun he would have with his father.

Adele had expressed her concerns to Sally about raising his hopes. However, Sally seemed to transfer her own need that things would work out onto Dean.

"Do you think he'll like me?" Dean asked as she zipped up his coat and tugged his toque down over his ears. He had asked this question several times, never wondering what Wyatt's wife would think of him. She probably didn't figure into his imaginings.

"You're a sweet boy," was all she could say.

"Will I stay here tonight?" He looked up at the house as she helped him out of her car, and it seemed the reality of what they were doing finally hit him. His smile shifted a bit, and Adele could see a flicker of uncertainty in his eyes.

"It's just a visit for now," she assured him, taking his hand.

She and Dean would stay in Millars Crossing tonight and visit the Sutton ranch during the day for the first few weeks. Ease him into the family, so to speak. Adele had booked three weeks off work—her entire block of holidays—but she knew she couldn't just drop off Dean and leave.

Not for the first time she mentally chastised her friend Sally for her casual attitude toward her son's paternity and his family. If she had been more honest and forthright, this would be easier.

Once Sally told Adele who Dean's father was, Adele had gone onto Facebook, Instagram, and Google and gleaned a few tidbits about Wyatt Sutton. He owned a ranch with his father and raised pure-bred cows. She found that out from a sales flyer she had discovered on Google. He had served on the Wheat Pool board and was a member of the Millars Crossing Chamber of Commerce. He'd also been involved in Millars Crossing Community Church's fundraiser last year. Nothing about his wife or children.

In the few pictures she saw of him, he looked solemn and serious.

Handsome in a rugged, I-don't-care-what-you think kind of way.

What if Wyatt rejected his son? Didn't believe her? What if it caused a huge rift between him and his wife?

Adele and Sally had thought of various scenarios.

So, Sally had written a letter, explaining the situation. And Adele had ordered a DNA paternity test kit.

But what would she do if Wyatt refused to take the test and wouldn't read Sally's letter?

She stopped her whirling thoughts. *One step at a time*, she told herself.

"This is a big house," Dean said, clinging to her hand.

"It is. Looks like a nice place." She caught the whiff of woodsmoke as they walked up to the large double doors flanked with sidelight windows. The windows were etched with horses, a nod to the animals that stood guard in the corrals beside the house. She had no idea when Sally said that Wyatt lived on a ranch, that it would look this...nice. Almost intimidating.

Adele took a deep breath, and with her heart pounding out an erratic rhythm, she rapped on the door.

Then waited, her nerves jangling, throat dry, trying to think of how to introduce herself and Dean. What to say to the boy's father? Wyatt's wife?

She waited another minute.

Nothing.

"Maybe no one's home?" Dean said, his voice thin, frightened.

Adele swallowed down a sob of despair. She should take this as a sign and head back to Whitehorse with him.

And then what? Park him in that crappy day care center, the only one she could afford, while she went off to work a job she hated, saving every penny for her own dream?

This was a beautiful house. It was out in the country. More than Adele could provide for him. And he would be with his father.

She knocked again, harder this time.

She finally heard a young voice calling out that he or she was coming.

The door creaked open, and a little girl with an unruly mop of copper curls stared at her. "Hi," was her simple greeting.

If Adele was uncertain of Dean's lineage, the color of the little girl's hair, the same as Dean's, reinforced what Sally had said.

The girl stared at them with unabashed curiosity. She wore a stained tank top, underwear, and nothing else.

Chocolate rimmed her mouth and she held the culprit, a half-eaten chocolate bar, in her hand.

"Hi yourself," Adele said.

"Who are you?"

"Is your daddy or mommy home?" Adele asked, dodging the question.

The little girl considered this, then, without another word, pulled the door open wider. "You come in," was all she said.

Adele glanced down at Dean to check his reaction. But he seemed intrigued, and he followed the child, which left Adele to follow him.

This wasn't the reception she had been expecting. Adele had read stories about kids getting dropped off on a doorstep, but they had always been in the point of view of the drop-ee, never the drop-er.

Which she was.

"Take your boots off, buddy," she told Dean before he went through another set of double doors.

The entrance held two long wooden benches, one on each side of the large space. A metal cradle holding some firewood flanked the door the little girl had just gone through. Coats and jackets spilled off one bench, boots scattered below it. Adele cleared a stack of newspapers and books off the bench on the other side of the entrance and sat Dean down, tugging his boots off.

He wasn't looking at her though, his eyes on the whimsical creature hovering in the doorway leading to the house.

"Where's your mom and dad?" Adele repeated to the little girl.

She said nothing, turning as Adele caught a flash of bright turquoise and glitter behind her.

Another young girl, identical to the first, joined them. The garish blue and pink princess dress she wore hung half open on her thin shoulders, its gauzy sleeves ripped. A tiara balanced crookedly on her own curls.

"Daddy's sleeping," the newest addition announced, frowning. "My mommy's gone." Adele tried to absorb what she was saying.

"Is your mommy coming back?"

"Nope. She's gone. Who are you?" she asked imperiously, as befit a princess. She directed her question and her wand at Dean.

"I'm Dean," he replied, his tone showing Adele he was genuinely curious now. "What's your name?"

"I am Maya, she is Maria," the princess said, her tone matter of fact, pointing a star-tipped wand to the chocolate-eating twin. "She is eating my candy."

"No. It's mine," Maria protested.

Maya's eyes narrowed as she raised her wand. It looked like she was about to bop her sister with it.

"How about we don't injure each other," Adele said, catching the wand before it connected.

"What do you want?" Maya asked, turning her attention back to Adele.

"I'm looking for your daddy."

"Come here," Maya announced, grabbing a handful of her too-large silky dress in one hand and scampering through the door to the kitchen.

Maria finished off her chocolate bar in one gulp and wiped her hands on her grimy tank top. "Come wif me," she commanded, following her sister.

Adele wasn't sure what to do, but Dean followed them, so she fell in behind.

As she entered the kitchen a horrible smell greeted her along with dark smoke billowing off a pan on the stove. Ignoring Dean's sudden cry, she ran to the stove and turned the burner under the frying pan off. A mass of black, congealed something stared up at her as she waved the smoke away. She flicked on the fan above the stove, hoping it would suck the smoke away, surprised the smoke detectors didn't go off.

What if she hadn't come in just then? What could have happened?

"What were you doing?" she asked the girls, her heart slowing as she drew in a calming breath.

"I was hungry," Maya announced, getting up on a chair pushed close to the counter.

"I can see that," Adele said, dropping the pan into one of the double sinks. The other one was full of dishes and cutlery. A bowl of soggy cereal and milk sat on the other side of the sink and a spilled box of dry cereal lay beside it. Broken eggs and remnants of shells littered the rest of the counter.

Although the kitchen was a minor disaster, Adele could see it was tastefully decorated with its narrow tiles on the back-splash and deep mahogany cabinets.

"Where is your daddy sleeping?" Adele asked, glancing around and trying to figure out what was happening in this home.

"He's on the couch," Maria offered, pointing to an arched

opening off the kitchen into a family room. The television was on, cartoons blaring out of the speakers.

Adele wondered how anyone could sleep through all this commotion.

She also wondered what kind of irresponsible father would sleep while his daughters were wreaking havoc in the kitchen.

What if he was dead?

Her heart stuttered in her chest as this horrible thought invaded her mind.

Grabbing Dean's hand, she walked him over to the kitchen table and made him sit down.

"Just stay here, honey." She turned to the girls. "You should sit down too. I'll be right back."

With a light shrug Maya jumped down from the chair by the counter and joined Dean and Maria, who was pulling out her own chair with a screech of the legs over the linoleum.

With another nod just to make sure they all understood, she sucked in a steadying breath and trudged into the family room, her heart pounding.

Please don't let him be dead.

And there he was, sprawled on the couch, a blanket draped haphazardly over him. One arm hung off the couch, his hand grazing the floor, his fingers twitching.

Relief flooded Adele. Still alive.

She moved closer, inspecting him.

Old memories of her own father, drunk and passed out on the couch, slithered into her mind. She fought down her revulsion and leaned closer, sniffing.

No alcohol. That was a relief.

His longish hair was a tangle, and damp curls clung to his forehead. He wasn't wearing a t-shirt and Adele was too aware of his muscular chest and arms. But then he groaned and turned, looking up at her, his brown eyes bloodshot and bleary.

"What...who..." he managed. Then his head fell back, his eyes drifting shut as he groaned.

Stubble shadowed his strong chin, creating a rugged bad-boy appeal.

Adele gave her head a shake, focusing on the matter at hand.

She laid her hand on his forehead. He was burning up with fever. She glanced around a room as messy as the kitchen. Papers and toys were strewn all over the floor. A few plates holding remnants of bread were stacked on one table beside some glasses still holding milk.

She wondered how long the girls had had free rein while their father lay there, ill. And from the state of this room and the kitchen, she guessed the house had been without a woman's touch for a while now.

Then Wyatt groaned again, twitching on the couch.

She couldn't leave him just lying there.

She shifted the blanket to cover him up better, then looked at the girls hovering in the doorway.

"Daddy's sick," Maria stated. "Can you make him better?"

"No. I can't." But she could at least give him something for the fever.

She gathered up the plates and glasses and brought them to the kitchen. She got her purse and rummaged through it, certain she had some ibuprofen or something similar.

Yes. There it was.

She washed a glass, filled it with water, and shook out a couple of pills for Wyatt.

He lay on the couch, eyes closed, hand flung over his head.

She understood how Sally could have been attracted to him. He was one good-looking man.

Again, she disregarded her foolish thoughts. She set the water and pills down and shook him awake.

He moaned then dragged open his eyes, staring at her.

"Theresa? You're back?" Then he frowned, swinging out one hand. "Go away. Go away now."

It seemed Theresa wasn't too popular.

One thing was for certain. She couldn't walk away from this mess.

What was going on?

A princess drifted into Wyatt's vision, turquoise and sparkly, waving a wand in front of him. He struggled to open his eyes, trying to grasp what was happening. His head pounded like someone was beating it with a sledgehammer, and his whole body felt like he'd had a bad go-round with a green bronc. A sense of urgency gripped him, but he couldn't sort out what he had to do.

Then a woman appeared, pulling a blanket over him.

Was Theresa back?

No. She was gone. Thank goodness.

Who was this, then?

Sleep and a dull nausea pulled him down into a crazy whorl of thoughts and worry. He was chasing cows that turned into blue butterflies and stars. Chocolate and kisses. His girls were dancing toward wild horses and he was trying to catch them.

Then, through all this, a woman with a deep husky voice was calling his name. Who was she? What was she saying?

He strained to understand her words, swimming upward through the heat that enveloped him and the unceasing nausea that made everything spin, including his stomach. He had to get up. He had things to do. But every movement triggered pain and whirling. Then a hand, soft and gentle, stroked his damp hair away from his face.

The voice sifted through the darkness that clung to him.

"You need to drink this," the voice was saying.

Was she part of these confused dreams? Wyatt blinked, trying to focus on her. A shimmer of wavy brown hair, gray eyes. A smattering of freckles that seemed to dance on her face.

She helped him to a sitting position and the dreams that had stuck to him slithered away for a moment, but the room spun around.

"Take these and drink them down," the pretty woman was saying, handing him a couple of pills.

Drugs? Should he take them?

"It's ibuprofen," she said. "It's okay." She held up one pill as if to show him.

His hand shook as he took the pills, his eyes flickering with vertigo. He dropped one as he tried to put it into his mouth, and she picked it up and placed it in his hand again. He swallowed and got them down without spilling too much water or throwing up. Then he laid his head back against the couch, exhausted by the effort, eyes closed to fight down the nausea.

"Can you stand up?" the woman asked him.

Could he? He tried to process this as he realized he was sitting on the couch in the family room wearing just his blue jeans. His T-shirt lay on the floor, his feet were bare. He blinked, looking around, and saw his daughters staring at him, smiling. They seemed okay.

Was this woman here to take them away?

"Are you with Theresa?" he managed. "You come to take the kids?"

"No. I'm not here to take the girls. Sally sent me here. She gave me your name and told me where you live."

He didn't know who Sally was, but the woman seemed concerned. She touched his forehead again, her hand cool. Soft. Gentle.

Then she was again urging him to stand so he could get to bed.

All he wanted to do was lie down again, but he knew he had to move.

He struggled to his feet, shaky and unsteady, wishing the room would settle down and stop its spinning as he stumbled alongside her to the bedroom.

He lay down on the bed and, with a groan, pulled his legs up, curling up, shivering with cold.

She pulled a blanket over him as he wrapped his arms around himself, trying to get warm.

Then, slowly, sleep pulled on him and he fell into another troubled dream.

CHAPTER TWO

*A*dele blew out her breath as she closed the bedroom door behind her. Wyatt was taken care of for now.

"I'm hungry," Maria called out as she walked toward the kitchen.

Obviously, that was next on the agenda.

Was there no one else around? No one else who could help him?

"So, let's make you girls some breakfast or some lunch," she said glancing at the clock on the stove. It was past noon already.

Time flies...

"What would you like to have?"

"I yike chocolate," Maria said.

"I can see that," Adele said. "But I'm not making breakfast out of something that's not a legitimate food group. How about I make you some French toast," she said noticing a few eggs left in the carton on the counter marooned amongst the shells and broken eggs. While she cooked, she could clean that mess up. "You three sit down and I'll get some lunch for you."

She found another frying pan, milk in the refrigerator, some bread in a bag on the counter, and mixed up some French toast for the crew. While that was cooking, she set out plates and cutlery. The girls didn't seem the least fazed by a complete stranger working in their kitchen.

Did this happen often?

With a guy as good looking as Wyatt? Maybe.

She wiped and washed and tossed and tidied while the French toast fried. When it was done, she placed slices on the kids' plates, pouring syrup over top. Maybe not the most nutritious meal, but it was all she could come up with based on what was available in the kitchen.

Which wasn't much.

How long has this been going on, she wondered, watching as the girls gobbled up the pieces of toast she gave them.

Maya gave Adele a broad, syrupy grin, wiping her mouth with the back of her hand before Adele could catch her. "Yummy in my tummy," she pronounced. Adele grabbed a tea-towel, dampened it, and wiped the girls' hands and faces, then handed it to Dean, who cleaned himself up.

"Oh no," Maria pronounced, her eyes wide, her hand over her mouth. "We didn't pray."

Really? Her father was lying in bed with a roaring fever, the house was topsy-turvy, they had been on their own who knows how long, and all she was concerned about was grace?

"I'm sure it's okay," Adele said, giving her an encouraging smile, thinking back to the scattered times Sally and Dean would pray for their food.

Maria shook her head, suddenly solemn. "No. We need to pray."

Maya was nodding along, her crown bouncing in her curls. "Daddy always does."

"Okay." Obviously, this was a priority.

Adele sat down beside the girls and folded her hands,

figuring it wouldn't hurt for now. She could manage some kind of prayer for the kids' sake. She used to pray, but she and God hadn't talked much since her foster father died.

"Thanks for the food," she mumbled. "And be with...be with Daddy. Help him get better."

"Amen," both girls pronounced, then jumped off their chairs.

"Can we watch TV?" Maya asked, her hands on her hips, her head jutted to one side as if expecting opposition from the adult in the room. Despite the circumstances, Adele had to laugh at the little girl. With her crooked crown and over-the-top princess dress, it was hard to take the little spitfire seriously.

She should say no, but she needed some respite from the kids to give herself time to process everything that had just happened.

And clean up this disaster of a kitchen while she figured out the next step.

"Sure you can," she said, giving in and ushering them into the family room. The television was still on, but she turned it down a few notches. For Wyatt's sake.

She looked over at Dean, trying to gauge how he was managing. She crouched down beside him, her hand on his knee. "So, how are you doing, buddy?" she asked, her tone quiet, calm, she hoped.

Dean just nodded, his attention on the television.

All the way down here all he could talk about was how excited he was to meet his daddy. His enthusiasm had worried her.

Worried her more than the tears he had shed after Sally's death.

"I'll be in the kitchen, okay?"

Again a quick nod and then a smile.

She should be happy he was so calm, but she wondered when this would all sink in.

She was having difficulty enough coping with the situation.

Not for the first time, she regretted her decision to bring him here.

But what else could she have done? What other options did she have? Sally had set this all up. Had told Dean, despite Adele's pleas to say nothing, that he would see his daddy when she was gone. Had made Adele promise, as she lay dying, to take Dean to his father.

Suppressing her concerns and worries, Adele returned to the kitchen. As she washed and tidied, she was pleased to see that overall the kitchen was more messy than dirty. However sick Wyatt was, and however long he had been sick for, he at least seemed to be able to keep the place clean. She wondered where his wife was. The mother of the girls.

But as Adele washed and tried to figure where to put everything away, she sensed the girls' mother either hadn't been around for a while or was gone.

Sadness gripped her at the thought. Poor motherless girls.

Which made her wonder who Theresa was.

Not your concern and not your worry, she reminded herself, focusing on the job in front of her.

When she restored the kitchen to some semblance of order, she went into the family room, tidying as she went. She brought a stack of kids' books back to the bookshelves, tidying the ones that were already there. She glanced back at the trio of children parked on the couch, eyes glued to the television.

Adele sat down beside Dean, slipping her arm around him, trying to give him some comfort. She was sure he was as confused as she was but couldn't articulate it.

He leaned into her hug, resting his head against her shoulder, which tore her up inside.

Why, Sally, did you make me swear to do this, she thought, the steady ache in her gut growing. *Why did you set Dean up for this potential disappointment?*

She looked at the girls, sitting slouched on the couch, staring at the screen, wondering what was going through their tiny heads. They seemed to accept her presence without too much concern. But it must be disconcerting to have a stranger in the house.

"What have we gotten ourselves into?" she asked, brushing a gentle kiss over Dean's head.

Her thoughts went to the man in the room adjoining the family room. What would he say when he found out about Dean?

Sally had told Dean before she died that he had a daddy who lived on a ranch and that Adele would take Dean to meet him. At the time, Dean was confused, but the more Sally talked about it, the more excited he got. He didn't realize that meeting his daddy meant losing his mommy. He was too young to put it all together. And all the way here he had seemed excited to see his daddy. That had made her feel better about the job she had taken on.

But now that they were here, could she walk away from him when the time came? Adele brushed that errant thought out of her mind.

You can't take care of him and you know it, she reminded herself.

She keenly felt again her lack of family. Neither her mother nor father had siblings. In fact, the only thing Adele knew about her mother was that she was the daughter of a single mother who had abandoned her. Her father's family lived overseas, and he hadn't been in touch with them since he left.

Nor had he contacted Adele since the last time he dropped her off at the Stefanskis', the foster family who took her in each time her father decided he couldn't take care of her.

Which all meant Adele had no backup to help her raise a child. Everything she'd learned about how a family functioned came from her foster parents, who were also out of her life.

Besides, she had promised Sally, and Adele prided herself on keeping her promises.

She cuddled Dean more, looking past him to the girls perched on the edge of the couch. Once the show was over, she should give them a bath.

And then what? What will you and Dean do? Stay here?

One thing at a time, she told herself, shaking her head at the strangeness of the situation.

Wyatt blinked, struggling to keep his eyes open. His head still felt tight and ached like he'd been pounded with an anvil. He still felt shaky, not sure if his thoughts were coherent or not.

All night he'd had twisted and troubled dreams of a woman bringing him water and pills. His daughters spinning in circles around him, making him dizzy. Trying to catch them as they ran away from him.

He lay there, testing his thoughts, thankful that the room didn't spin as much as before. Then he looked around, frowning. What was he doing in the spare bedroom?

He sat bolt upright in bed.

Maria, Maya? Where were they? What had happened to them while he was out of it? He pulled the damp sheets away from him, shivering in the sudden chill as he realized he still wore his blue jeans. But no shirt.

He yanked open the door of the room, then leaned against the frame, spots dancing before his eyes as weakness and nausea washed over him again. Taking a breath, he looked around the family room. But the girls weren't on the couch, watching *Paw Patrol* or just about anything that sang, danced, or moved.

Where were they? Outside?

Dear Lord, no. It was full-blown winter out there.

He dragged himself up the stairs, stumbling toward the girls' bedroom, sweating with the effort, his head spinning. He pushed open the door, his heart pounding, hoping, praying.

Then relief flooded through him.

They both lay in Maya's bed, curled up together, their arms wrapped around each other like they'd been when they were new-born. Didn't matter how many times he moved them in the night, they would find each other and sleep together.

He eased out a sigh and sent up a prayer of thanks as he clung to the door, trembling with the fever that still gripped him.

How long had he been out of it? All he could remember was stumbling into the house after doing chores, stripping off his shirt because he was hot. After that it was just a blur of pain and debilitating nausea.

He mustered what little strength he could and staggered over to their bed, dropping beside them, stroking Maria's curls away from her forehead. Her hair was soft and silky. It felt like she had washed it. Maya wasn't wearing that ridiculous princess dress she had insisted on wearing ever since she had found it in a bag of clothes that Alicia Mays had given him at church on Sunday.

Now they both wore pajamas, and they smelled good. Maria lay curled up, spooning with Maya, who was sucking her thumb.

He stroked their hair, catching his breath, wishing he didn't feel so weak.

He pressed his hand to his still aching head, trying to corral his confused thoughts.

He had vague memories of a woman helping him to a bedroom. Giving him pills.

His heart stuttered again as that thought dropped through the fuzz in his brain. He didn't know her. Was she still here? How did she get here?

Struggling to his feet, he staggered out of the bedroom,

holding on to the wall as he went. He first checked his bedroom, across the hall, but the bed was still made.

He checked the room his brother Reuben used to sleep in, then Finn's former room, but no one was sleeping in them either. Finally, he came to his sister, Carly's room.

And there she was. The woman who helped him, fast asleep in his sister's old double bed, a little boy who looked to be about five years old curled up beside her. Her brown curly hair spilled over the pillow, her dark lashes a crescent against her freckled cheeks.

Who was she and why was she here? And who was the boy?

As if his thoughts drifted into her mind, he saw her eyes open slowly then look around the room, looking disoriented. Then she saw him, and she jolted upright, clutching the blankets to her chest. Her long brown hair was a tangle, her gray eyes wide.

Part of his brain acknowledged the fact that she was exotically beautiful

"What? What's going on?" she gasped, staring at him with wide, unfocused eyes.

"I think that's my line," Wyatt said.

The woman blinked, blew out her breath, then laid back down on the bed, her arm over her eyes.

"Can you please leave and let me get dressed, and I'll tell you what's happening."

Wyatt's eyes skimmed to the little boy in the bed, the curve of his cheek, his copper curls teasing out a memory that he couldn't grasp.

He gave the woman a tight nod, closed the door. Then he made his way downstairs to make some coffee. Hopefully that would clear his brain.

CHAPTER THREE

*A*dele's fingers trembled as she tucked her shirt into her blue jeans. Thankfully there was a mirror over the dresser in the room, and she finger-combed her hair, looking at her reflection. She ran her tongue over her teeth, wishing she had her cosmetic bag.

Of course, this little sleepover wasn't supposed to happen. This visit was supposed to be a quick hello, an introduction, however awkward that might be.

Then she and Dean were supposed to head back to the Airbnb in Millar's Crossing and spend the night.

Instead, she had bathed the three kids, put the girls in their pajamas and tucked them into bed, trying to figure out what they were saying when they told her she had to do prayers with them. She knew Sally sang a prayer with Dean every night. She remembered the tune but not the words, so she just hummed it. That seemed to be enough to satisfy them. Adele decided to put Dean to bed at the same time, and he was too tired to protest.

She was once again surprised at how he seemed to just go

with the flow. Adele envied him that. That had never been one of her strengths, although it would've been a good coping skill, given what she'd dealt with in her life.

She took another deep breath, wet her finger, and cleaned out some of the smudged mascara from underneath her eyes, wishing again she had brought something to tidy up with.

Doesn't matter, you're not trying to make any kind of impression on him. You're just here for Dean.

And with that self-talk ringing in her mind, she opened the door and walked down the carpeted hallway to the stairs.

In the kitchen, Wyatt sat at the table, his hands cupping a mug of steaming coffee. Thank goodness he was wearing a shirt this time. The memory of his bare chest could still make her feel a bit swoony.

"Coffee's on," he said with a nod toward the pot that was burbling on the counter.

The smell made her mouth water, so she walked over to a cupboard, grabbed a mug, and poured a cup for herself.

"There's cream in the fridge if you want," Wyatt told her. "I think. Not sure."

"I'm fine. I just drink it black."

She stood a moment, feeling awkward, and figured that now, while the kids were still sleeping, would be a good time to get some of the weird stuff out of the way.

She sat down at the table. "So, I'm sure you're wondering who I am." She looked over at Wyatt, who was staring at her. To her dismay, her heart did a little trip in her chest. Despite his pale and drawn features, he was even better looking in real life that he was in the grainy pictures she'd seen of him on the internet. Solid jaw, shaded with stubble that only added to his appeal. Dark eyebrows over deep-set eyes. Narrow nose and perfect cheekbones. Hair so thick and tumbled it made her want to reach across the table and rearrange it. Run her fingers through it.

And as she looked at him, she glimpsed Dean's parentage. Dean had the same narrow nose, the same eyes. She didn't know if she was being objective or projecting, but regardless, Wyatt was an attractive man.

She pulled herself back to reality. She wasn't there to admire Wyatt's looks or be distracted by them.

"I am wondering who you are," he said, massaging his temples with his fingers. He still looked ill. "How did you get here? How did you know..."

His eyes drifted shut as she sipped on her coffee, trying to corral her thoughts and slow the nervous beat of her heart.

While she was thinking, he waved to the counters that were now sparkling clean. "I suppose I have you to thank for that?"

She nodded, gripping her cup with chilly hands. "When I got here things were pretty much a disaster."

"I'm guessing Maya tried to make eggs?"

"I think that's what she was trying," Adele said, taking a sip of her coffee. She wished her heart would stop pounding. Wondered if he could hear it from across the table.

"Do you mind telling me what happened yesterday? If it was yesterday?" He closed his eyes, massaging his temple with his thumb. "My brain is all mixed up and fuzzy."

Adele ran her finger up and down the handle of her mug, trying to collect her thoughts. Trying to sort through them and find what to say first.

"I came here yesterday, and the girls answered the door. Things didn't look too great..." Which was the understatement of the year, she thought, but no sense beating him up while he still looked so bedraggled. "The girls were hungry, so I gave them something to eat, and then I cleaned up." Adele bit her lip, smiling a little at the strangeness of the conversation. Again, not at all what she had thought of or what she had rehearsed all the way down here.

"You were on the couch, somewhat delirious," she continued.

"You kept talking about cows and some woman named Theresa, and the girls. I could tell you were in rough shape. So I gave you some ibuprofen I had in my purse. Then took you to your bedroom because I figured you would be more comfortable there."

Wyatt shook his head. "I have no idea what happened. All I remember was coming in from chores feeling sicker than I've ever felt in my life. I had the girls with me, and I was trying to get them to change from their chore clothes into regular clothes. And then while they did that, I sat on the couch. And that's all I can remember." He looked over at her with a pained expression. "I wasn't drunk. I... I..."

"I know," Adele said, feeling a glimmer of sympathy for the man's obvious discomfort. "I could tell as soon as I came in the living room that you weren't well."

He took another sip of coffee, then sat straighter, looking as if he was trying to gain control. "So. Who are you and why are you here?"

The moment of truth.

Adele paused, glancing behind her, listening. "I don't want the kids to hear..." her voice trailed off, concerned.

"I don't know how your little boy sleeps in the morning, but the girls will be solidly out of it for the next two hours."

She pulled in a breath and shifted so she could monitor the stairs and Wyatt at the same time.

"Okay. My name is Adele Marten. The little boy with me is Dean." She swallowed, wishing she could still the thudding of her heart. Slow the rapid beat that threatened to choke her. "He's...he's your son." She paused, letting those ominous words settle.

"Say what?" Wyatt frowned at her, his eyes blinking as he tried to absorb what she was saying.

"He's your son. Sally Henshall is his mother. I had hoped to call you and let you know I was coming, but neither Sally nor I had any information for you. No phone number. Only the town where you lived."

"Sally Henshall," he repeated slowly, his confused frown deepening. He shook his head. "I don't remember anyone by that name."

This was a problem she thought might come up but hoped wouldn't.

"She told me you two had been together. In Mexico," she said, pressing on. "And Dean was the result of that."

He looked at her, his expression growing hard. "No. No way. I'm not taking this on. I don't believe it. I don't believe you."

Adele swallowed, thinking of Dean and how excited he was to see his father. Should Sally have told him? Should she have followed through with this?

"I'm not lying. Dean's mother, Sally, knew your name and that you lived in Rockyveiw on a ranch with your father and brothers. She told me your one brother was named Reuben-"

"She could have found that out anywhere," he snapped, interrupting her. "And if I'm his father, why didn't she tell me sooner?"

He sounded angry, and while Adele couldn't blame him, her own frustration grew with the situation. *I didn't ask for this,* she wanted to tell him.

But then, neither did he.

"She was going to, but then she found out you were married." As soon as she spoke the words, she realized how lame they sounded. "She was afraid of disrupting your family."

"I would be afraid too," he said, pulling in a deep breath. "It's a lie. She would have had some information on me if we'd spent any amount of time together."

She sucked in a breath at his bald declaration. "I have a letter that Sally wrote to you naming you the father. Explaining the situation."

"That proves nothing. Anyone can write a letter full of lies."

"Sally wasn't a liar." Her own frustration spilled out into her voice. What would she do if he didn't believe her? What would happen to Dean?

"I told you, I don't know who this Sally is." He sighed. "I may not be well, but I'm not that sick."

"What if I showed you a picture of her?"

Wyatt closed his eyes, dragging his hand over his face. He looked like he was fading again. "Sure. Go crazy."

Adele got her purse and pulled her phone out. She flicked through her pictures, her heart flickering at the sight of her old friend. She found the best picture of her. One with Dean when they are both smiling and happy.

She expanded the picture and brought her phone over to Wyatt, laying it on the table in front of him.

Wyatt set his elbows on the table, resting his chin on his hands as he looked down at it. He blinked again, then rubbed his eyes and shook his head. "Sorry. I got nothing."

Annoyance flared through her at his quick dismissal. "You met her in Mexico. At Welks Resort in Cabo-"

He snorted. "Of course I did."

She ignored his sarcastic tone. "It was in September. You were there on a holiday with your brother. A wedding."

Wyatt pushed the phone back across the table at her. "I was there all right, and yes, I was with Reuben, but that proves nothing."

Adele wanted to press him. He wasn't feeling well, so he probably couldn't think straight. Maybe once he thought about it for a while he would remember.

She had to believe Sally. What would she do otherwise? Go back to Whitehorse with Dean?

"Sorry to cut this conversation short, but I have work to do," he said, pushing himself to his feet. "Thanks for taking care of the girls. I'm sorry you had to stay the night. I can't thank you enough for that."

"Of course. I couldn't leave them or you in the lurch."

Wyatt nodded, then winced, his eyes slamming shut, as if fighting pain. "So, I'll gladly pay you-"

"No. Please don't." There was no way she would accept money from him.

"So what will you do now?"

And wasn't that the question. If he wouldn't acknowledge Dean as his son, she had another plan she was hoping she wouldn't have to execute. It would require Wyatt's cooperation, and from the way he looked, she doubted she would get it.

"Del? Where are you?"

Dean's sleepy voice broke into the silence that had dropped after his question.

"Over here, sweetie," Adele said, jumping out of her chair and hurrying to the little guy's side.

His face was still flushed from sleep, a faint line from the sheets marking his chubby cheek. He smiled at her, burying himself in her hug.

"Did you have a good sleep?" she asked, brushing his hair back from his face.

"I did. I was afraid when I woke up. You—you—you weren't there." His faint stutter made her smile even as it created more concerns.

"I'm sorry, buddy. I should have been. You must have been a bit afraid waking up in a strange house."

"Just a—a—a little." His wide smile showed her all was forgiven.

She stroked his cheeks and pressed a quick kiss to his head, then turned to Wyatt. He was staring at Dean as if trying to place him. His eyes were narrowed and for a moment Adele thought he would acknowledge him. But then Wyatt's gaze slipped to Adele and his mouth grew tight.

"So, this is Dean." His voice was hard as he spoke the words, and Adele heard the condemnation in them. She realized how it looked from his side of the situation. As if he had been ambushed.

Which he had been. Not for the first time she wished she'd had some way of connecting with Wyatt earlier so she could have prepared him. Wished Sally had connected with him.

And what difference would that have made? Clearly none.

However, time wasn't her friend in her current situation. She needed to get Dean settled in the next week or so.

She was supposed to meet Leah in Edmonton at the auction sale in a couple of weeks. Their plans were in place and she couldn't change them now. No matter how much she wanted things to be different, there was no room in her future apartment, or her life, for Dean.

Then Dean looked over at Wyatt, his smile growing shy. "Are —are—are you my—my daddy?"

Adele's heart fell like an icy rock into her stomach. Why, oh why, had Sally encouraged this little dream? Why had she told him?

Adele had tried to hold her friend back, but when Sally was dying, she was determined to tell Dean about his father.

And now?

She could see Wyatt's jaw clench as he looked at Dean. She saw his struggle with his emotions.

Then he turned to Adele. "Sorry, but you'll have to leave. I've got to get my girls and then go feed my cows."

He walked away from the table and then slowed, his steps uneven, wavering. He reached for a chair as he teetered, then on his way down, cracked his head against the back of the chair and crashed to the ground.

"You're lucky you didn't get a concussion."

Dr. Brent Williamson made a notation on the chart, then set

it down, shoving his hands in the pockets of his lab coat, frowning at Wyatt.

"You don't get a concussion falling on the floor," Wyatt managed as he buttoned up his shirt.

"But you could by hitting a chair on your way down," Brent said. "Good thing someone was with you." His eyes slipped to Adele, who hovered in the opening of the examining room, the children clustered around her. She had dropped him off at the hospital, then gone to get more ibuprofen. Now she was back and watching with a concerned expression.

"But his head is okay, isn't it?" she asked.

"He's got such a hard head, I think he could hit it with an anvil and be okay," Brent said with a chuckle as he glanced from Adele to Wyatt.

Wyatt could almost hear the questions grinding through his friend's head.

Questions he had no intention of answering or addressing right now. He was hanging in there, his head pounding, and feeling shakier than he had this morning.

"So, there's nothing else you can do for him?" Adele asked, her hand resting on the shoulder of the little guy standing beside her. The girls didn't seem as concerned as he did. But then the twins were always interested in seeing new places, meeting new people. "He's really sick."

Wyatt stared at Dean again, trying to figure out what to do about this kid that Adele claimed was his.

"As far as I can tell, it's a virus," Brent said. "And there's nothing we can do for a viral infection. Time is the only solution for them."

"How much time?" Wyatt managed as he tried to stand, fighting off a wave of dizziness.

"Whoa, take it easy, cowboy," Brent said, catching him as he wavered. "As for time, we've seen a few more cases of this flu.

It's a bad one. Most people seem to fight it for at least a week. Sometimes two."

Wyatt didn't have a week or two. He barely had one day, let alone two. Too many things to do and less than zero energy. Reuben was coming back to the ranch in a few months, and he had to get things ready for the expansion.

Finn was making noises about coming back as well.

Too much going on.

And now he had to deal with a kid this lady said was his.

He caught his balance, then reached for his coat. Spots danced in front of his eyes again, and he held onto the bed, waiting for the dizziness to pass.

Then Adele was beside him, helping him with his coat, making him feel even more foolish than he already did. He hated feeling this weak, especially in front of this beautiful woman.

"Well, let's get you back to the truck," Adele said. She hovered as he struggled to button up his coat. Thankfully she didn't help with that.

"Just make sure he gets lots of rest and drinks lots of liquids, but don't let them talk you into going horseback riding." Brent chuckled, and Wyatt ignored his comment. A couple of years ago he had taken Brent riding, and it hadn't gone well. Brent never let him forget it every time he saw him.

Adele didn't bother following up on that comment and walked beside him as he slowly made his way out of the hospital. The first blast of cold air felt good on his heated face, and then he began shivering again.

As the door fell shut behind them, he stumbled, and once again Adele caught him, her arm around his waist supporting him, draping his other arm over her shoulders.

"I'll be okay," he muttered.

"The sidewalk is covered with snow. There's no way I'm having you fall and dragging your sorry self back into the emergency room again." Adele sounded businesslike and a bit snappy, which, despite the circumstances, made him smile.

"You sound like you could be a pretty bossy person," he managed, leaning on her as they walked back to his truck.

"When I need to be, yes. I can."

The kids trailed along behind them, chattering away as if they had been friends for years.

Adele pressed the key fob, the truck lights flashed, and then she opened the door. Thankfully Wyatt clambered in by himself. Not elegant, but he managed. He rested his throbbing head on the backrest, wishing he was back home in bed, wishing he had the mental space to wrap his head around what was going on in his own family.

Later, he told himself. When he got back, he had to feed the cows.

Adele got the kids into the truck and buckled them up. She climbed up into the driver's seat, started it up, and a few moments later they headed out of town, driving to the ranch.

The kids had been quiet in the back up till then.

"Are you sick?" Maya asked him, her voice unusually quiet.

"Your dad is not feeling well at all," Adele told her, her hands clenching the steering wheel as she drove. "But he'll get better soon."

Wyatt drew in a long breath, turning his head to look at her. "You look tense. Have you never driven a pickup before?"

She bit her lip, shaking her head as she slowed to make a turn onto the road leading to the ranch. "I've ridden in one enough. But I've never driven one."

For a small moment he wondered what she meant by that, but he was too tired to follow up on it.

Maya and Maria seemed content with Adele's answer and soon were asking Dean questions. Wyatt tried to focus on what they were saying, but his head was so tired it was just a bunch of jabbering that poked at his sore brain.

Finally, they made it back to the ranch. Adele parked the truck and got the kids out while he tried to open the door and get out himself. Clinging to the door handle for support, he got out without falling. And then Adele was there, once again supporting him.

"You have to take me to the tractor," he said, trying to head to the corral, fighting his weakness. "I need to get hay to the cows."

Even the thought of walking that short distance sapped what little energy he had left. But he had no choice. The cows would be hungry.

"You're not driving a tractor in this condition," Adele said, ignoring him, leading him to the house.

"Okay. But later today it needs to happen."

"Of course," was all she said. She opened the door to the house and let the kids in. He followed, dropping onto one of the benches by the door.

She made quick work of stripping boots, mitts, toques, and coats off the kids while he gathered his energy to push his boots off.

The kids scampered away as he struggled with his coat. Adele just stood and watched him, allowing him to manage on his own. Having her help him with this would be too humiliating.

"I'll grab a nap, and then I'm feeding the cows," he insisted, in case she forgot.

Adele nodded, then helped him as he got to his feet.

"You need to take more ibuprofen and some vitamins, and then back to bed," was all she said.

He wished he had enough strength to protest, but he was tapped. So he did what he was told, then staggered back through the family room, heading for the spare room.

The kids were playing with some blocks at their table and barely spared him a glance as he passed them. At least they were occupied.

He dropped onto the bed, unable to think of doing anything more.

"Just let me sleep for a while, then wake me up," Wyatt said. "I need to feed those cows today."

"Don't worry about those cows. Just make sure you get some rest."

Wyatt closed his eyes, unable to say another thing. Once again, he found her cool hand on his forehead, and then she was tucking the blankets up around him like he was a little kid. He didn't have the energy to protest and fell into a fitful sleep.

CHAPTER FOUR

*A*dele watched Wyatt to make sure he settled down. When he closed his eyes, she left the room.

The kids seemed content to play with the wooden blocks, laughing as they tried to make the tallest tower possible.

Once again, she was surprised at how easily the girls took Dean into their circle. And he seemed more than happy to play with them. Did they know on some level that he was their brother? Was this a hopeful sign of things to come?

She shook off the thought.

Right about now she didn't dare think too far ahead.

Through the windows past the children, she could see cows gathered around a feeder. Wyatt was concerned about them and she wondered what she should do about that. He was in no shape to head out today. But could the animals wait until tomorrow?

You know how to run a tractor. You could feed them.

She let the thought settle, looking behind her at the room where Wyatt lay. He was so weak yet.

She pulled in a breath then made a quick decision.

Her foster father had always said that animals depend on humans to take care of them. Right now it was cold outside, and she knew how important it was for the animals to be fed.

"Hey kids, let's go for a tractor ride," she announced. Even as she did, she hoped there would be enough room for them behind the tractor seat in the cab.

If there wasn't, they would have to squish in. She couldn't leave any of them here in the house by themselves.

This time when she got them dressed for outside, she put the girls' snow pants on. She had remembered to pack Dean's in the car when they left the Airbnb yesterday. Another thing her foster parents had always pounded into her. Anytime she headed out in the vehicle, they always made sure she packed toque, mitts, and snow pants. The one time she had deemed it unnecessary, she had hit the ditch and was stranded for a couple of hours, freezing with bare hands, thin blue jeans, and no toque.

She never forgot after that.

It was still snowing outside as they walked down the driveway toward the large shop where Adele assumed the tractor was parked.

She stepped inside the building and her heart dropped when she saw how huge the thing was. Did she really think she could drive it?

From the looks of the size of the cab, all the kids would fit.

She pulled on the chain, hand over hand, to raise the large overhead door. Cold air swirled inside the heated shop. At least the tractor was warm.

"My turn by the window," Maya announced as they walked toward it.

Adele didn't know which window she was talking about. The cab had windows on all sides. But they clearly had a plan as she climbed up the narrow steps to open the heavy door.

She helped the twins up the stairs, and Maya scooted behind the driver's seat to a makeshift bench on the housing, covered with a blanket. Maria sat beside her then looked past Adele to Dean.

"You sit between us," Maya announced, pushing her sister over and making room herself. It was a bit tight, despite the size of the tractor. Adele was sure the manufacturers didn't figure on three little children as passengers, but it worked.

"You girls are amazing," Adele said with a grin as she set herself in the seat, familiarizing herself with the controls. There were lots of them, but she understood the basic ones.

With another quick prayer, she turned it on, and with a roar and a plume of smoke billowing out of the exhaust, the tractor started. It chugged along, knocking for a few minutes, and then another roar and it kicked down.

She eased it out of the shop to let it run for a few minutes outside, letting it warm up. While she did, she looked around the yard, scoping it out. She saw the piles of hay bales she would need to retrieve, noticed where the gate was that she'd have to go through.

"Okay, kids, I need to get out to close the door," she said.

"Don't touch anything," Maria interrupted her, holding up a finger. They must have been told this before.

She had to smile as she got out. She made quick work of closing the door, then got back in.

Scootching up on the seat to reach the pedals, she put the tractor in gear, backed up, and headed toward the bales. It took her a bit to figure out the controls for the front-end loader but soon she had a bale loaded and was headed toward the gate.

A few moments later, she was out of the tractor and opening the gate, watching the cows with a wary eye. When she helped her foster father feed the cows, she was always terrified that they would come barreling towards the open gate, heading for freedom.

But Earl would just laugh at her, reassuring her that the last thing the cows wanted was their freedom. They were hungry, and even if they got out, they would follow her back to the feeders.

She drove through the gate, shut it behind them, and clambered back up in the tractor again. Seriously, she thought, this climbing up and down the stairs would be a workout.

She drove toward the feeder, then had to slow down as the cows gathered around the tractor. She got the bale dumped into the feeder, pleased at how well it went.

"Does your daddy have a knife to cut the strings?" Adele asked, turning back to the kids who were sitting there, looking around, quite content to just sit. *Good kids*, she thought.

"Up there," Maria said, pointing to where a leather sheath was screwed up beside the doorway. Adele grabbed the knife out of there, then turned to the kids. She had to leave the tractor running again.

"Remember what we talked about before? You kids have to stay exactly where you are," she warned, underlining her statement with the lift of a finger. "Don't touch a thing."

"No touching," Maria repeated. "Daddy says so too."

"You guys know the drill," Adele said, wondering again about the girls' mother. She guessed she was gone, but how long? Had she died? Had she left?

She doubted she would find out soon.

"I won't touch anything either," Dean assured her.

"Thanks, buddy. Do you mind keeping an eye on the girls for me while I go outside?" She didn't like having them stay in the tractor, but it would be even more dangerous to take them outside with the cows milling around. *Best bad choice*, she told herself. "Just make sure they stay behind the seat."

Dean nodded, giving her a careful smile.

She held his eyes, feeling a rush of sympathy for the little guy. His whole life had been upended the last couple of weeks, and now he sat in a tractor with two girls he had never met before, who were presumably his sisters. He seemed to take it all in stride, but she guessed there would be a day of reckoning for him.

She tried not to think too far ahead as she got out of the tractor. Tried not to think what might be in store for him.

For now, the cows needed to be fed.

Roll with the flow, roll with the flow.

These words had been her mantra most of her life. Every time her father decided he couldn't stick around anymore, and he dropped her off at the neighbor's place, he would repeat these words to her. She was never sure if they were a warning or a comfort. But either way, they became ingrained in her subconscious.

She climbed up into the feeder and made quick work of cutting the strings, pulling them off, thankful they weren't frozen to the bales. As she did, she remembered the many times that she would tug strings loose on bales when she fed cows with Earl. She would have to yank and pull, taking large hunks of hay along with the strings. She had worked in bare hands in minus twenty-degree weather, the wind howling, being pelted with snow as hungry cows gathered around her.

Helping on her foster parents' ranch was expected. But she didn't mind. She loved the work, loved helping Earl with all the chores around the ranch. Loved being outside and working with animals. They had even trained a horse together. When Earl died and her foster mother, Bonnie, had to move, it was another wrenching, horrible twist in her life.

Another loss and another painful reminder of the vulnerability that being connected to people caused.

And the pain that came with each loss.

Adele shunted those thoughts aside, focusing on the job in front of her. She wound the strings around her hand, tied them off, and carried them to the tractor.

While she worked, she kept her eye on the kids. They had taken her warning to heart and stayed where they were, watching her.

She climbed back in the tractor, turning to smile at them. "You guys did real good. Thanks for being such good listeners. We just have to do this a few more times."

She wasn't sure how many bales to feed. She just figured she would put as many bales in the three feeders as they would hold and check them tomorrow.

If she was still here.

An hour later, the cows were all munching on their hay, gathered around the three feeders, and Adele was parking the tractor in the shop.

Maria had pulled her mittens and toque off and Maya had unzipped her coat. She got them all dressed up again and took them one by one out of the tractor.

While she closed the door, the three of them ran toward a pile of snow beside the door of the shop. They were climbing up and sliding down on their butts, laughing and giggling as they tossed loose snow at each other.

"Okay, guys, we should get to the house," Adele called out. She wanted to check on Wyatt and make sure he was still okay.

"We want to play outside," Maria called out. "We're having fun."

"I can see that," Adele said with a chuckle. Maya had piled snow on Maria's head, but they were both laughing. Dean was burying his legs in the loose snow, his cheeks rosy and his eyes bright.

Adele thought of the last three days of driving he'd endured. The poor kid was ready to have some physical activity. And the girls looked like they were having fun.

"Let's first go up to the house. I just want to see how your dad is feeling," she said.

They grumbled but followed her anyway. There was another

pile of snow beside the parked vehicles, and while the kids climbed up and down that, Adele went inside.

She didn't bother taking her boots off. The snow on them was clean and she could wipe it up later.

Wyatt lay on his back, still fast asleep. She watched him a moment, thankful to see he wasn't as restless as he had been before.

His hair lay across his forehead, his dark lashes fans on his stubbled cheeks. Even fast asleep he was attractive.

And don't even think about going there.

Adele had learned the hard way that good looks did not automatically mean a good person. Troy was as good looking if not even better looking than Wyatt. He had promised her the world but had broken her heart.

Besides, she was just here to get Dean settled in, then she had to get back to Whitehorse. She had plans, and they didn't include any man. She and Leah would finish what she and Sally had started.

A bakery. And it would be amazing.

This had been a dream of hers for years, and while it broke her heart to know Sally was no longer involved in the plans, Adele was thankful she had found a partner in Leah. Thankful that it was all happening soon.

The kids were squealing and screaming, sliding up and down the hill, still laughing when she rejoined them outside.

Adele pulled a metal chair from beside the door, brushed the snow off of it, and sat down to watch them.

The metal was cold on her behind, but she didn't mind. It did her heart good to see Dean playing with the girls.

Once again, she was struck by the fact of how easily they connected with each other.

It was as if they knew they were related.

Adele folded her arms, stretching her legs out in front of her, wishing she knew what to do next. Wishing, once again, that she had her foster mother to talk to. Wishing she had someone to talk to. Leah was more business partner than confidant.

Sally had been her closest friend, and she was gone.

She swallowed down a knot of sorrow, blinking away the tears. She couldn't give in to her grief now. Her focus was Dean. Getting him settled in.

And trying to convince Wyatt that this little boy was his.

Wyatt opened his eyes, looking around the dark room, testing the pain in his head. It had eased somewhat. Still there, but less than before.

Slowly he sat up. The room wasn't whirling like it had and for the first time in a couple of days, he felt as if he could walk without wavering.

He wondered what time it was. Either evening or early morning. He wasn't sure which.

His heart jumped in his chest.

The girls. Were they okay?

He shot to his feet and the room spun again. Spots danced in front of his eyes as he waited to get his balance.

Struggling, he made it to the bedroom door and opened it. And there she was. The woman who had danced in and out of his fevered dreams. Talking to him with her husky voice. Asking if he needed anything.

In other dreams she was touching him, holding his hand, leading him through fields that turned into rocks he was stumbling over. She was calling him to come to her. Always, beside her, was a little boy.

Now she sat on the couch, holding a book in one hand, sipping something from a mug she held in the other. A frown of concentration pleated her forehead as she read. She put the mug down, turned the page, and coiled a strand of her brown wavy hair around her finger.

She was even prettier than she was in his fevered imaginings.

As if sensing him gazing at her, she looked up, frowning. Then she put her book down and stood, rubbing her hands over the legs of her blue jeans.

"How are you feeling? How's the head?" she asked.

"A bit better, and the head is fine." He pulled in a slow breath, wishing he could tell her the truth.

That the room still spun and that he couldn't figure out how he would make it from the doorway to the couch without looking like he was drunk.

"Do you want some tea? Coffee?"

"Tea, probably." He stayed where he was, clinging to the doorpost for support, but trying to not look like he was clinging to the doorpost for support. "Where are my girls?"

"They're still sleeping."

"What day is it?"

"Wednesday morning, if that helps."

"I need to feed my cows."

How he would manage that, he wasn't sure, but they'd needed hay yesterday. He was surprised he wasn't hearing them bawling in protest yet.

"You don't need to worry about them," she said, giving him a tentative smile that settled into his fevered brain. "I already did that."

"You fed my cows?" He frowned, trying to absorb what she was saying.

"I gave them about eight bales yesterday, based on the size of the feeders. Is that enough?"

He just stared at her, confused.

"I can give them more today if I need to," she said quickly, mistaking his hesitation.

"No. No, that's perfect." He shook his head, then regretted the motion as he made his way to the couch, frustrated that he still felt so lousy.

"How did you know what to do?"

"I know my way around a tractor."

He wanted to ask her more, but his head was still fuzzy. Adele watched him, her frown deepening. "You still don't look too great."

He laid his head back against the couch. "Thanks a lot." Though he was relieved the cows were taken care of, he wished he felt better.

"Wasn't meant to be an insult," she said, a note of humor edging her throaty voice. It was a nice voice, he thought. Soothing. "I'll go make that tea."

She left and he heard her moving around in the kitchen through the ringing of his ears. It sounded cozy. Like when his mom was alive. A few moments later she was back with a pot of tea in one hand and a mug in the other.

"Sugar? Milk?"

"No. Nothing." He rarely drank tea. That was Theresa's particular habit. He was surprised there was any left. She'd been gone for over two and a half years.

"How are you really feeling?" she asked again as she poured him a cup.

"Confused." He took the mug, cradling it in hands that were now chilled. "I don't know who you are, other than your name, but you fed my livestock, took care of my kids and..." He paused, thinking of the little boy she had come with. "And if I remember correctly, you've got some little boy that you say is mine."

Dean, he remembered. The kid that Adele insisted was his. And what was he supposed to do about that? The kid was here in the house and seemed to think he was his father. Who would do that to an innocent young boy?

"So far so good," she said, her voice tight, as if she was holding back some emotions.

"Did the tractor start okay?" he asked, preferring to focus on more practical topics for now.

"Yes. The shop was warm, but I plugged it in when I was done just to be safe. It's cold out there this morning."

He took another sip of his tea. He was thirsty. Hadn't had enough to drink despite waking up to glasses of water by the bed. Left there by her, he suspected.

He leaned forward, cradling the mug in his hands, absorbing the warmth. He wasn't as shivery as he had been.

"Do you need another ibuprofen?" she asked.

"Sure." Hopefully it would help.

"Can I make you something to eat?"

He tested that thought. He wasn't hungry, but if he didn't eat, he wouldn't get better.

"Maybe some toast? I hate to ask, but it would take me longer than it would take you."

"I know my way around your kitchen," she said, getting up again.

He watched her through the opening between the family room and kitchen as she worked. She seemed to know where everything was.

A few moments later she was back with a plate heaped with golden eggs, perfectly scrambled, and a piece of toast as well as a couple more pills. "I know you said just toast but thought you might like some eggs."

"Thanks. This looks great," he said as she set it on an end table beside him.

He took the pills with his tea, then started in on the eggs and toast, surprised to find out how hungry he was. As he ate, she settled down on the opposite side of the couch, looking comfortable.

Considering she'd already been here a couple of days, it shouldn't be too surprising.

He ate his eggs and toast and she sipped her own mug of tea. Thankfully, she didn't see the need to fill the silence with conversation. Right now, he was still trying to process everything that had happened the last couple of days. Which wasn't easy given how sluggish his brain felt.

But when he was finished with the food she'd given him, he had to admit he felt better. He picked up his mug of tea and leaned back, sipping it, grateful again for the silence.

However, he knew it couldn't last. Things were just too strange right now.

"Forgive me, but I can't remember who you said Dean's mother is?"

"Sally. Her name is Sally Henshall."

Still didn't ring a bell. "She's your friend?"

"Was my friend and roommate," Adele returned, tucking her feet under her as she relaxed in the opposite corner of the couch.

Right. He remembered that Adele had said Sally had died. "Sorry about that."

Adele acknowledged his apology with a tight nod.

Another moment of quiet, then he plowed on. "How long had you known her?"

"I met her when Dean was two. We were both looking for a roommate, so we moved in together." She clutched her mug close, taking another sip of tea.

Wyatt rubbed his forehead again, struggling to think. "And she told you I was the father?"

"Not right away. She said nothing about Dean's father at all. Only that she had gotten pregnant on a trip to Mexico."

Mexico. Wyatt barely remembered that trip as it was. A destination wedding for a friend. He didn't want to go, but his brother Reuben, who was the best man, figured it would do

Wyatt good to come along. He and Theresa had just broken up for the third time. So he went. It was a wild week.

He remembered spending a lot of time at one bar. Something he had been doing far too much of at that time, even when he was home in Millars Crossing. It was the time of his life that he was the most ashamed of. He knew he had been drinking in Mexico. Knew he had gone to a couple of parties. But he couldn't remember the woman whose picture Adele had shown him.

Of course, his brain wasn't firing on all cylinders right now.

With a shrug, he finished the rest of his tea. "I wish I could remember. That would make things easier, but I can't."

Wyatt set his empty mug aside, crossing his arms over his chest, thankful he was feeling more focused. "What's your plan? For being here...for Dean..."

"We're staying at an Airbnb in Millars Crossing. I had figured on us staying there overnight and then my bringing Dean to the ranch every day this week."

"So I could get to know him better?"

"That, and something else I think we need to discuss."

"There's more?"

Adele nodded as she ran her finger up and down the handle of her mug. Wyatt recognized the mug as one of a set he and Theresa had received as a wedding present from Reuben and his wife, Denise. The only reason he remembered them was because Theresa had mocked them.

"I guessed you would have your questions about Dean, and that's to be expected," Adele said. "For all you know, I could be anybody with any kid stopping in at your place. You need to know this wasn't my idea. Sally pleaded with me to bring him here. Besides, I had hoped you would remember Sally and being with her..." Her voice trailed off and Wyatt could see a faint flush staining her cheeks, bringing the sprinkling of freckles across her cheeks into relief. She took a breath, tossed back her hair, and looked him directly in the eye. "But just in case that didn't happen, I bought a DNA test kit. To make sure."

She stopped, her flush deepening.

"A DNA test kit," he repeated, pulling in another breath.

"Like I said, I had hoped you would remember for Dean and for Sally's sake, but this would be a backup."

He fought down a surge of frustration at the condemning tone in her voice.

"Well, if Dean was mine, I would have hoped that this Sally person would have had the decency to contact me sooner."

"You're right," she said, holding a hand up as if to pacify him. "Trust me, I've had many conversations with her about telling you. I kept encouraging her to let you know. But she said she'd waited too long. By the time she was ready, she found out you were married, and she didn't want to cause any problems."

"Maybe because Dean isn't mine." But even as he spoke the brave words, he remembered what the little guy looked like. How familiar he seemed.

He shook that off. *The power of suggestion,* he told himself.

Adele looked down at her mug, quiet for a moment. She licked her lips, keeping her eyes downcast. "I only know what Sally told me, and she wasn't a liar." She pulled in another breath. "I don't know how she could've gotten your name other-wise. We lived all the way up in Whitehorse. How in the world of all the men in this country would she have chosen you?" She looked up at him, as if challenging him.

Wyatt tapped his fingers on his arm, letting her words regis-ter. There was a spark of truth in that. And yet...

"I guess we'll never know why she did that. Now that she's gone."

Adele pressed her lips together, blinking. Wyatt could see a lone tear slide down her cheek, and he cursed himself for being so insensitive. Despite what was going on now, Sally had been her friend, and he had no right to be callous about her passing.

"I'm so sorry," he said. "I shouldn't have said that."

"I think we're both feeling a little emotional right now."

Wyatt wasn't sure what he was feeling, but he sure wished the fuzziness in his head were eased away so he could focus better.

"I've just got too much going on," he said with a sigh. Which reminded him, he had to call Reuben soon. Make plans for his return to the ranch.

"I'm not trying to judge you or anything," Adele said, holding his gaze with her soft gray eyes. "But what happened when I came here? The girls were on their own. Where is their mother?"

"Theresa, their mother, left us a couple of years ago," he said, bitterness still edging his voice. "She didn't like living on the ranch, and she didn't want to take care of twins. Her own daughters."

"So you've been on your own with the girls ever since then? I understood from what Sally said that you were ranching with your father and your brothers."

As her comment registered, he felt a niggle of unease. "How would Sally have known that?"

"Because you told her?"

Uncertainty dogged him. *Why could he not remember Sally*, he wondered, his mind skipping back to that trip.

"At any rate," he continued, going back to her questions, "my father passed away the same year I married Theresa. And my brother left a year and a half ago, after his wife died. Said he needed some time away." Wyatt rubbed his temples with his index fingers, trying to ease away the headache that still gripped him. A headache that grew with each conversation he had with Adele.

"I'm so sorry to hear about that. You've had a rough go," she said, a note of sympathy in her voice.

Wyatt lifted one shoulder in a shrug, not sure what to say to that. Losing his father had been like a body blow to the family. And then to watch his brother deal with Denise's deteriorating health, it was just too much.

The time away had seemed to help Reuben, and he said that he wanted to come back and work on the ranch. Carly, the baby of the family, had left when her fiancé broke up with her. Just before he went to jail.

As for his other brother, Finn had kind of lost his way after their father's death and embarked on an around-the-world trip. The last anyone heard from him, Finn was in Bangkok, living on a beach.

It had been disheartening to discover how jealous Wyatt was when he found this out. How he wished he could just up and leave, dumping all his responsibilities on the one left behind. Except there was no one left behind but him. Holding the fort for the family and taking care of his children. Watching the family that had once been so close, disintegrate, broken by events beyond anyone's control.

"I take my responsibilities seriously," was all he could manage.

"So you were taking care of the girls all by yourself?"

Wyatt shook his head, then regretted the action. "No, I've had a nanny come in every day since the girls were born, but she took some time off. She needed to take care of her mother after her surgery." Not that Ruby did a lot. Basically took care of the kids during the day. For the rest, he and the girls had been on their own. He made dinner, put them to bed, tried to keep the house from getting too messy. Which was like trying to brush your teeth while eating Oreos. He never felt like he got ahead of the cleaning, the laundry, and trying to get the girls to bed on time.

"In other words, you *have* been taking care of the girls all by yourself," Adele repeated.

"I have," Wyatt said. "Except for two days ago. That was a

major parenting fail." He shuddered, thinking how close things could have come to a true disaster. The girls on their own in the kitchen with a stove.

"You couldn't help being sick," Adele assured him.

"I'm just thankful you showed up when you did," Wyatt said with a small smile. "I don't know what the girls would have gotten up to if they'd been unsupervised any longer."

Adele set her empty mug aside, crossing her arms. "I'm also glad I showed up then, even though I wasn't coming with the best news."

Her comment created another heavy beat of silence.

And what was he supposed to do about that?

"What's your plan for today?" Wyatt asked.

"Dean is asleep, and once he wakes up, he and I are heading back to Millars Crossing. I need to get some clean clothes and have a shower."

"Sure. Of course." He glanced at the clock. "I'm hoping the girls sleep longer." He would manage with them around. Somehow.

"Oh, right. The girls." She bit her lip, as if thinking. "I can take the girls with me and then come back with them and stick around for the day. To help out. Unless you'd rather I don't come back for a while to give you a chance to rest some more."

He wanted to protest, but he was still feeling shaky despite the breakfast. He had to be realistic and do what Reuben had often accused him of not doing. Accept help when it was offered. "No. That'd be great. I don't know if I can take care of the girls myself yet." The tension in Wyatt's shoulders eased just a little bit at the thought of her help. "I know I wasn't the most welcoming when you first came, but I sure appreciate you lending a hand."

"I'll be coming every day, so if you need any more assistance with the girls, I don't mind sticking around during the day."

He paused, then released a laugh. "Again, that would help.

The nanny said she would be back in a couple of weeks, max. She told me she would let me know if it was any earlier."

"I can help you out for a little bit," Adele said. "But I need to be in Edmonton in a week and a half."

"What for?" He wondered if she would take Dean with her. Or would she leave him behind?

"I'm going to an auction," Adele answered, breaking into his thoughts. "It's for bakery equipment."

"You have a bakery?"

"Not yet. I am hoping to start one in Whitehorse. Sally was going to be a partner..." She paused, biting her lip again. Once again Wyatt felt a surge of sympathy for her. Despite the fact that she had literally dropped on his doorstep with a little boy he knew nothing about, none of this could be easy for her either. Losing her friend then having to hike all the way down here. Something else occurred to him.

"Just putting this out there, and please don't take any offense," he said, leaning a bit closer. "But you never thought to take care of Dean yourself?"

She turned away from him, her expression growing sorrowful.

"You seem to care about him," he pressed, curious now. "He seems attached to you."

"He's your son," Adele said. "He needs to be with you. That's how family works."

She got up, grabbed his plates and utensils, and strode back into the kitchen, leaving him with more questions than answers.

CHAPTER FIVE

*A*dele stood by the sink, breathing in and out, stifling the guilt that Wyatt's comment created. The thought of taking care of Dean herself had often floated through her mind. But after Sally had told Dean about his father, after she had begged Adele to bring him to Wyatt, she knew she had to respect Sally's wishes.

But she didn't have to like it.

"I'm sorry," she heard Wyatt say as he came into the kitchen. "I shouldn't have said anything. Your relationship with Dean is none of my business."

"It's okay. It's a legitimate question, and you have a right to ask," Adele said, turning the tap on. She started washing up the mugs and plate, keeping her back to him. "Especially since I'm thinking you should take care of him..." She let the sentence drift away, realizing she needed to talk to him and explain.

She heard Wyatt sit down at the kitchen table and knew he was waiting.

When she had put the mugs away, she turned to face him,

crossing her arms over her chest again. Defensive posture, Sally had always told her. The kind of move that usually turned men off.

Not that Adele was looking for a man to be with. After Troy, she'd had a few guys waft in and out of her life, temporary, unwilling to commit. Just like Troy. The North drew men who were just passing through. Men like her father.

Nope. She was making plans to take care of herself, thank you very much.

"I love Dean a lot. And it breaks my heart to leave him here," she said. "But I made a promise to Sally to take him to his father, and if there's one thing I've learned in my life, it's that family needs to be together." To her immense embarrassment, her voice quivered.

"And you think I can give Dean that family?" Wyatt drew in a long breath, as if trying to figure out how to have this discussion. "I don't want to be a jerk, but I knew nothing about him until the day before yesterday."

"I know. And I appreciate that. I recognize this is disorienting for you, but what I think doesn't matter. Since Sally told him about you, he's talked about nothing else but meeting you." Adele blinked, looking away, wishing she could be more realistic about this.

Wyatt sighed, rested his elbows on the kitchen table, and looked around. "I grew up in this house, you know," he said quietly.

Adele wasn't sure where he was going with this, but decided he had earned the right to think aloud. She sat down across from him, waiting.

"I used to imagine raising my family here. I knew I would take over the ranch someday. Me and Reuben had always talked about that."

"Reuben's your brother, right?"

"Yeah. He's younger than me but not by much. Finn is

younger than him, and then there's Carly, our sister." He leaned back in his chair, looking around the kitchen, as if remembering other times. "I had dreams and plans. I was going to marry someone who wanted to work beside me on the ranch. We would have four kids. Two boys. Two girls."

"Well, you've got a good start on that family," Adele put in, giving him a cautious smile. She didn't mention that he only needed one more boy to get his dream family. Dean was still a variable for him.

Wyatt nodded tightly. "Yeah, seems like." He pulled in a heavy sigh, massaging his temples. He gave her a wan smile. "Anyway, I appreciate you taking the time to help me out. Hopefully our nanny comes back soon."

His smile created a surprising warmth deep in her stomach. Created an unexpected and unwelcome yearning for family and home.

It's a myth, she reminded herself. But even as the old words, often thrown at her by her father, sifted through her mind, behind them came images of her foster family. How they were always willing to take her in. Give her a home each time her father dropped her off.

Which made Bonnie's defection after her husband died all the harder to take.

She shook her head as if to dislodge the memories. She was a big girl and more than capable of taking care of herself. Dealing with whatever life threw at her.

She hesitated, feeling awkward, but then thought of Dean and the limbo his parentage seemed to be in.

"So, two things. I have a letter Sally wrote. I think you should read it. I don't know what she said, but it might help."

Wyatt pursed his lips, then gave a shrug. "Sure."

"And the DNA test..." She paused, hoping he would finish.

Wyatt drummed his hands on the table, looking weary. "I

guess I owe you, so I'll do it. It would answer your questions, at least."

She almost sagged in relief at his acquiescence. She thought she would have to push harder.

She waited to see if he would say anything more, but he slapped his hand on the table and sucked in another breath as if he had made a sudden decision. "Let's do my part right now," he said. "I'd like to get this done. You can take Dean's swab when he gets up and take it into town when you go. You can send it registered overnight mail. If you get there before five o'clock it'll go out today. I'm sure it will be at the lab by tomorrow. Maybe you can call them and ask for a rush job. I'm willing to pay more if need be. I don't want this hanging over me any longer than necessary."

As if to underline his words, he closed his eyes, clutching his head. "I got to get back to bed. I need to shake this flu."

He got to his feet and wavered. She moved in immediately.

"I'm okay," he muttered, clinging to the back of a chair.

Despite his claims, she still felt the heat emanating from his body. The fever hadn't broken yet. "That may be, but I'm helping you anyway. There's no way I'm driving you back to the hospital again. I'd have to wake the kids up and pack them in the truck, and that would be awful for them, and you would be in bed and I'd be dealing with cranky kids." She knew she was nattering, something else she did when she was nervous.

She blamed it on the tension of the past few days, but if she was honest with herself, part of her nerves had to do with being so close to this man. Feeling the ripple of his muscles as he moved alongside her, the weight of his arm on her shoulder.

She tried to dismiss her thoughts. Push aside her reaction to him. She was just here as a favor. He was only putting up with her because right now he needed her.

As she helped him onto the bed, he looked up at her with a hesitant expression. "Sorry to ask even more of you, but do you mind getting me some clean clothes? I've been in these too long and I could use a change."

"Of course. I don't mind at all."

"My bedroom is-"

"I know which one is yours," she said, then realized how that sounded. And before he could make any comment about that, she scurried out of the room.

Even though he had asked her, going through his closet and dresser felt invasive. She noted that he preferred button-down shirts. That he had a preponderance of plaid. That he seemed to like wool socks. He had an entire drawer full of them.

Everything was clean and neatly folded. He was a tidy person. For some reason that raised him in her estimation. She caught a whiff of some cologne as she went through his clothes. Woodsy, masculine. A scent that reminded her so clearly of her ex-boyfriend it created an unwelcome yearning deep within.

Though it had been two years since she had walked away from Troy, the loneliness she'd felt after he left still bit.

He doesn't deserve your sorrow, she reminded herself. *He's not worth it.*

She swallowed, lifted her chin, and grabbed a shirt, pants, and whatever else Wyatt needed, then, just before she was about to leave, she stopped by a wall holding a variety of pictures.

She knew she should leave but she couldn't stop herself.

There was a picture of him with his daughters outside, posed in front of a stand of trees blazing orange and yellow. The sun shone down on them, warm, kind, and they were all smiling.

There were a few more of the girls, cute candid shots. One on a fence, both of them perched on the back of a horse.

Then, down in one corner of the gallery, was Wyatt with a young woman who stood beside him, pregnant. His wife, she assumed, and probably carrying the twins. She stood with her hands on her hips, her chin up, a curious expression on her face. Her hair, gray with streaks of pink, was cut in a short bob.

Adele studied her, another sliver of sorrow shivering through her.

Why had she left? What had happened? And, even more puzzling, why would a mother leave her daughters behind?

It's not your concern, Adele told herself, clutching the pile of clothes and leaving the room.

Yet as she walked past the girls' room, she risked a peek inside to see if they were still sleeping.

Though Adele had put them in their own beds, they were now curled up together on Maya's. She smiled at the sight, then closed the door and checked on Dean.

Also fast asleep. She watched him a moment, her heart twisting in her chest. Could she walk away from him?

How would he be treated? What would happen to him here?

She closed the door, laying her now-aching head against it. She couldn't think that far ahead. For now, she wanted to ease him into this new phase of his life.

And if he wasn't Wyatt's son?

The insidious thought snaked through her mind and she quashed it.

He was. He had to be.

❧

"What are we doing here?" Maya asked as Adele parked in front of the Airbnb she was staying at in Millars Crossing.

"I just have to grab a few things, and then we're going back to the ranch," she said. The kids had been patient when she stopped at the post office to mail off the DNA test kit. Dean was curious when she swabbed his cheek this morning, but she'd told him it was to make sure he wasn't sick like Wyatt was.

The man working behind the counter was incurious about who she was. He quickly weighed the package and told her what it would cost for next-day delivery to its destination. She hoped it would come back as quickly. Wyatt had paid extra for rush results.

Now she had to make one more stop and then back to the ranch.

She sure hoped Mrs. Flikkema wasn't home. She didn't feel like explaining what was happening.

The kids followed her up the sidewalk to the side door.

"Okay, kiddos, I need to have a shower," she said, setting them down in front of the television and turning it on. The last time it was on, Dean had been watching *Paw Patrol* on Netflix, so it showed up immediately. "Can you sit here and watch television for a few minutes?"

Maya tapped her chin, as if thinking, then gave Adele a quick nod. "We'll be good."

Adele held her gaze a moment, as if making sure, then glanced over at Maria, who was already settling in on the couch.

"I'll make sure," Dean put in with a serious look.

"Thanks, buddy."

She grabbed some clean clothes and washed up. She knew Dean would be okay, but the girls worried her.

Her hair was still wet when she stepped out of the bathroom, but a quick glance around the room showed her everything was well.

"Maya tried to play on your laptop but I told her she couldn't," Dean announced, not even looking up from the television.

"Thanks, Dean. That was good babysitting," she said, toweling off her hair. It was cold in the suite but she hadn't been able to turn the temperature up. She guessed Mrs. Flikkema had it set so that occupants wouldn't turn the thermostat up too high.

"I'n not a baby," Maya announced, shooting Adele a frown.

"No, you're not," Adele agreed, finger-combing her damp hair. She wasn't sure she should take the time to blow-dry it even though it was cold outside. Though the kids were still watching television, she could tell they were getting fidgety. Maya was bouncing in place and Maria was yawning and rubbing her eyes.

She pulled her hair into a damp ponytail, grabbed her laptop and sketchbooks, and shoved them in her backpack. She wasn't sure how much time she'd have to work on her bakery plans, but she hated being without the option.

"All right, you guys, time to go," she said. To her surprise, Maria came running up to her and grabbed her hand. The little girl grinned up at her, swinging her hand. Again, so accepting.

"Are we going to the ranch?"

"I need to get groceries," Adele said, giving her an apologetic smile. They'd been great, and she knew she was pushing them to the limits of their endurance.

"Okay," she said with a dismissive shrug.

Adele got their coats, mitts, and toques on, thankful they were still cooperating. As she zipped up Dean's coat, he frowned at her. "Are we staying at the ranch tonight again?"

"No, honey. I just needed to get a few things. We'll be coming back here."

Dean frowned. "I like it better at the ranch. It's funner than here."

Adele felt a glimmer of sympathy for him but was happy to know he enjoyed being there. "I know, honey. But we'll stay at the ranch during the day. You can spend time with Maya and Maria when we're there."

That seemed to satisfy him. He gave her a smile, then released her hand.

She got the kids out the door and out to the truck.

Shoot. She'd forgotten her backpack. "Hey kids, sorry, I have to get one more thing yet. I'll be right back. Don't get into anything," she said as she helped them into the truck.

She hurried back to the house, let herself in again, ran to the couch, and picked up her backpack. She turned the television off, checked to make sure nothing else was on, then scooted back out of the house. Just before she got to the truck, Mrs. Flikkema appeared in front of her. Adele gasped, startled, her hand on her chest.

"I'm sorry. I didn't mean to scare you," Mrs. Flikkema said, holding her hand up as if to soothe her. "I just wanted to make sure everything was okay."

Adele shot a quick glance at the truck, but as far she could see the kids were still all buckled in. She turned back to Mrs. Flikkema. "Everything is fine. I'm just headed out for the day."

"I see that. I didn't think you had a truck," Angie said, waving to the vehicle parked on the street. "I thought you had a car?"

Nosy much. Adele wanted to brush her off but figured that would be rude.

"I do..." She hesitated, not sure how to get herself through this potential quagmire. "But I just-"

"Are those the Sutton twins in your truck? Wyatt's kids?"

Guess Millars Crossing was smaller than she thought.

"Yes. That's who they are." Her mind chased fragments of ideas, trying to figure out how to spin the situation.

She may as well get as close to the truth as possible.

"Funny thing happened the last couple of days," she said with a smile she hoped looked more sincere than it felt. "I had to visit Wyatt Sutton as a favor for a friend, and he told me his nanny was gone and he was looking for some help. Dean gets along well with the girls, so I thought I would help him out."

She gave Mrs. Flikkema a bright smile, as if this was the most normal thing in the world. To come visiting a town, and then get a temporary job. Why not?

And she was skating close enough to the truth that anything Mrs. Flikkema might hear would reinforce the scenario she just laid out.

Mrs. Flikkema didn't need to know what was going on in

her life, and she wanted to make things as easy as possible for Dean and Wyatt. So this was the best story to go with for now.

Angie Flikkema nodded, as if absorbing this information. "Yes, I know he's been stuck when the kids' nanny left him to take care of her mother. She's been with him since Theresa took off. I still can't believe that woman left him in the lurch like that." She shook her head as if commiserating with Wyatt's situation. "That man, actually, that family, has had a tough go the past few years."

Her curiosity was piqued, but Adele knew she couldn't allow Mrs. Flikkema to indulge in the gossip she wanted to impart.

The kids were in the truck and she didn't dare leave them alone too long.

She edged away, hoping Mrs. Flikkema got the hint. But the woman moved closer, warming to her topic.

"Theresa was nothing but trouble," Mrs. Flikkema said with a tight nod of her head. "I know there's been a few people who saw her out and about with other guys. And her with two little kids at home. She was brazen."

"I'm so sorry to hear that. I'm sure that must've been difficult. But the kids are in the truck... I need to go." She was getting too much information for her liking. She had to stop this, hoping the kids wouldn't overhear. "Take care, and I'll be back tonight."

She strode away, hoping and praying that Mrs. Flikkema wouldn't follow her. She dropped her backpack on the front passenger seat of the truck and walked around to the driver's door.

Mrs. Flikkema was right behind her, opening the back door and poking her head inside. For someone who ran a Bed and Breakfast, she had few boundaries.

"How are you kids doing? Having a fun trip into town? Nice for your mom that she could get a job here," Mrs. Flikkema said to Dean. Her bright eyes skipped from the twins to Dean and back again as if hoping she could find out something more.

"I'm sorry, but we have to get going. I also need to get some groceries." Adele almost face-palmed herself. Why was she giving this woman so much information?

But this seemed to satisfy Mrs. Flikkema. She stepped back from the truck, closing the door.

"Will you give my greetings to Wyatt?" she asked, folding her arms over her chest. "And hopefully I'll see you some time tonight. Nice for Wyatt to have help, that's for sure."

Adele didn't like her smirk or the way she had made her last comments. As if Adele had other plans up her sleeve other than being a nanny to Wyatt's kids.

But again, she wasn't about to encourage the woman anymore. So she just nodded, got into the truck, turned it on, and drove away, tossing a quick wave over her shoulder at Mrs. Flikkema, who was watching them leave, her arms crossed.

Adele wondered if she would rush back to her house as soon as they left and get the gossip mill going.

Don't think the worst. It'll all be fine, she said to herself as she turned toward the grocery store.

At the grocery store no one acted like they knew Wyatt's twins.

Half an hour later she was pulling up to the ranch, parking beside her little car.

It took her a few trips to get everything in the house. Wyatt wasn't inside, and she hoped he was okay. He was still shaky this morning. Once everything was put away, she figured she might as well take the kids outside and see if she could find him.

It took her a bit to get the kids dressed up to play in the snow, but they were patient with her tugging and zipping. Finally they headed out, the girls squealing like monkeys that had been let out of their cage.

"Can we go sliding?" Maya called out to Adele as Maria and Dean tossed snow at each other.

"Where?"

"I know where," Maya said, and without another word took off across the yard, Maria right behind her.

Dean, once again, was right with them, laughing as they ran.

"Hold off," Adele called out when she heard the tractor approaching the yard. Wyatt was probably feeding the cows again. "I hear your dad in the tractor."

They waited for her and she scurried to catch up, grabbing their hands.

"Snow over dere," Maya said, pointing with one mittened hand.

"Let's go sliding," Maria called out when she saw the pile of snow by the shop. She ran ahead of them, her toque askew. Maya was right on her heels.

But Dean held back this time.

"It's okay, buddy, you can go with them," Adele encouraged him. He hesitated another moment and then, sensing something was wrong, Adele knelt down in front of him. "What's the matter, sweetie?"

"For how long are we staying here?"

"I'm not sure." She wished she could tell him more, but things were still so uncertain.

"Are you staying with my daddy?"

Adele's heart twisted at the question.

"Dean, come play," Maya called out, saving her from replying. For now.

"Why don't you go play with the girls," Adele said, cupping his cheek with her hand. She gave him a gentle kiss, then, satisfied by her gesture, Dean ran off to join the girls.

The twins were already clambering up the pile, squealing and laughing, their voices echoing around the yard. The sun shone, creating sparkles on the snow, catching twinkling glimmers of light from the snow the girls tossed about.

Adele stood back, watching, smiling at the sight of Dean playing with the girls. Despite their unfinished conversation, he seemed happy.

For a moment she envied him. If all went well, he would stay here. And if it didn't? If the results came back negative?

She slammed a door on those thoughts. She didn't dare think that far ahead. Sally couldn't have led her wrong.

The ponderous drone of the tractor's diesel engine grew louder, and Adele glanced behind her to see Wyatt driving the tractor up to the gate.

"You guys stay here," she called out to the kids. "I'm going to help your dad."

The kids just nodded, more than content to stay where they were. Adele jogged through the snow across the yard and got to the gate just as Wyatt did. She made quick work of unlatching the chain hooking the gate together and swung it open, the gate screeching as she did. Wyatt waved his thanks, then drove through. She waited till he was on the other side then closed it up again.

Wyatt drove the tractor to the shop and again she was ahead of him, pulling on the heavy chain to open the large overhead door.

He drove it inside, the roar of the diesel echoing in the large shop. She let the door down, the chain clanking as she did, checking on the kids just before the door slid down. The kids were oblivious, sliding up and down the hill on their snow pants, still laughing and having a great time. The door slid shut and she couldn't see them anymore.

Wyatt got out of the tractor and pulled off his gloves, walking over to her.

"Thanks for the help," he said. "You know your way around the ranch."

"I've opened enough gates and enough shop doors. I know the drill. Stay a few steps ahead of the tractor and out of its way."

He smiled at her, and to her dismay that smile once again dove into her soul.

"Someone gave you good advice," he said, shoving his gloves in his pocket. His brown eyes held hers a moment longer than necessary, as if wondering who had.

For a beat, she couldn't look away.

"You must be feeling better," she said.

"Yeah. A bit. Get tired too quick, but at least I'm on the right side of everything. Thanks again for helping. I'm glad you're here."

She blinked at the kindness in his voice. At the sincerity. It created a yearning deep in her soul.

"You're welcome," she said, still unable to tear her gaze from his, not sure where to put these uncertain feelings. And he didn't seem eager to break the connection either.

"The kids seem to be having fun," he said.

"They get along well," Adele said. And she felt like smacking herself. It was as if she was trying to say something more.

"Kids are easygoing with the big things in life. They hit the bottom hard and then bounce back."

Adele wondered if he was referring to his wife's defection. Her mind slipped back to Mrs. Flikkema's comment about Theresa. She wanted to ask him more about her, but knew it wasn't her place.

Besides, things seemed to be shifting between them and she had to be certain to maintain proper boundaries. It would be hard enough to leave Dean behind; the last thing she needed was to leave another piece of her heart with Wyatt.

"How did things go in town?" he asked as he opened the door for her.

"I got the package away express post. I'll give the lab a call tomorrow to make sure they got it. And then I guess we'll wait and see."

She tried to keep her tone noncommittal and conversational. Tried not to think how much rested on that DNA test. Wyatt's future. Dean's and hers, if she was honest. If Dean wasn't Wyatt's child, Adele knew there was no way she was letting him be put into foster care. She loved the little boy too much.

But you can't take care of him.

Once again an unconscious prayer slipped into her mind. It was comprised of two words.

Please, Lord.

It was all she could manage right now.

At one time she and God had been close and her prayers had been longer than these panicked, half-formed requests she had been winging heavenward.

But life had beat her down, and so many prayers had gone unanswered that she didn't trust God much anymore.

"Well... That's good. We'll just have to wait and see then." Wyatt was chewing on his lower lip, and Adele wondered what was going through his mind. A lot hung in the balance for him.

"Daddy, Daddy," Maya called out, standing at the top of the snow pile. "Watch me go down on my pants," she yelled. She dropped to her seat and then slid down the hill, arms up, squealing with laughter.

Wyatt laughed at the sight, and Adele was surprised at the sound. And at the way his laughter transformed his face.

"Oh, baby girl, you are something else," he called. He walked over to her and grabbed her in a big tight hug. Maria slid down the hill to join them and was also pulled into his arms.

Dean stood to one side, watching the little group.

Adele's heart ached for him. She walked over to him and gave him a hug.

"Group hug, group hug," Maya called out, dancing from one boot to the other.

She ran over and grabbed Dean's hand, dragging him into the circle. Dean still held onto Adele's hand so she got pulled in as well. There was a flurry of arms and squeals and hugs and to her dismay, in the melee, Adele ended up right beside Wyatt.

"Daddy give a group hug," Maya demanded.

Wyatt and Adele's faces were inches apart, their eyes holding. A frisson of awareness shivered down Adele's spine. The moment lengthened and then Wyatt blinked, looking away.

"I should go back to the house," he said, his voice gruff.

Adele avoided his gaze.

"We want to play outside," Maya insisted, pulling away from her father and heading back to the hill.

That suited Adele just fine. Right about now she had to clear her head. She wasn't blind. She knew that something was building between her and Wyatt. She couldn't let it happen. She had to keep her focus on her plans.

She had to take care of herself.

No one else would.

CHAPTER SIX

*W*yatt closed the door behind him and leaned against it. What was he doing? He wanted to blame that moment of weakness a while ago on the sickness that still gripped him. Sure, Adele was an attractive woman, and her helping him out put him in her debt.

But he couldn't allow these ridiculous feelings for her. He blamed it on the loneliness and the moments of desperation when he felt like he couldn't take one more day of handling everything on his own.

He pushed himself away from the door, toed his boots off, and hung his coat on one of the racks. He had to plow the yard out yet, but feeding the cows had tired him out. Besides, it would be safer to plow the driveway when the kids were back in the house.

As he looked around the entrance, he had to smile. The entrance was tidy, and when he walked into the kitchen it felt like home again.

Ever since Theresa left, he'd felt like he was barely staying on top of things. The house was always a disaster, and the kids were always a royal mess, even with Ruby Mulder, the nanny, helping out. She was good with the kids, just not so much with the housework.

But now the kitchen was tidy, the house smelled good, and the kids were outside, laughing and having fun.

It created a sense of peace he hadn't felt in a long time.

He walked into his office just off the kitchen and dropped into his chair, turning the computer on. He logged into his bank and checked his bank balance. Not for the first time he felt the clench of anger at the state of his accounts. It had cost him so much to satisfy Theresa's demands.

And now he had other financial challenges to deal with.

The last time he spoke with his brother, Reuben had mentioned coming back to the ranch. Legally it was one quarter his, one quarter Finn's, one quarter Carly's, and one quarter Wyatt's. They knew Wyatt was building up the ranch after paying out Theresa, so none of his siblings had ever pushed him to pay them out of the profits. Their ownership was a reality he still had to deal with but only owning one quarter of the ranch had benefited him when it had come time to settle the divorce with Theresa.

That and the fact that she had left the girls with him.

He still couldn't believe the heartless gall of her. Leaving her daughters behind. Walking away from them. What kind of mother does that? What had he ever seen in her?

As his mind skipped back to Theresa, he thought of Dean's mother, Sally, and her claim that he was Dean's father.

And what was he supposed to do about that? How could he deal with that on top of everything? All he could do was hope that the DNA test would prove he wasn't the father.

He sat back in his chair, the headache that had dogged him for the past few days shifting and exerting pressure on his brain. Once again, he struggled to remember his time with Sally. He had never been with any other woman other than Theresa. If they had been intimate, surely he would remember that? But why would Sally have made this up?

Maybe when he felt better the memory would come back?

He wanted to go lie down and lose himself in sleep, but he'd done enough of that the past few days. He had to get to work.

With a sigh of resignation, he clicked through his accounts, paying a few bills that had come in, pleased to see the account still holding its own. The calf crop was good and this year he didn't have to buy hay.

When he was done, he checked the weather. The forecast wasn't great. Snow and wind, which meant he should get the driveway plowed if more snow was coming. Adele needed to get back to town tonight.

He heard the chatter of the kids' voices as they came near the house, and despite how lousy he felt, he had to smile. It was good to know they were enjoying themselves. Since Theresa left, guilt had been his constant companion and, knowing the twins were—for now anyway—cared for, eased the burden he'd been packing around ever since Ruby left a week ago.

And what will you do when Adele leaves?

He got up, shaking that thought off. For now, things were flowing along and that would have to be good enough for him. Ruby would be back. Sometime.

Adele was taking Maria's boots off when he joined them on the porch.

"We had fun sliding," Maya yelled, jumping on the bench, her cheeks bright pink, her eyes shining.

"I'm right here, honey," he said with a smile at her loud exuberance.

"I know. But I had fun," she repeated, in case he didn't get it the first time.

"That's good. I'll be making that pile bigger tonight," he said, tugging her boots off. "I have to plow out the yard and driveway."

"Yay. I'm happy," Maya said, wiggling with pleasure.

"Will you have to put a blade on the tractor to do that?" Adele asked, her husky voice creating, again, that unwelcome thrill.

"Yes. It's a quick-attach." He rolled his eyes as he pulled off Maya's coat. Why did he think she would be the least bit interested in that bit of information?

"Nice. You don't even have to get out of the tractor," she said, obviously knowing what he was talking about. She hung up Maria's coat and set her snow-encrusted mitts, toque, and scarf aside. Then she helped Dean finish taking his outdoor clothes off. The kids scooted out of the porch, eager to go onto the next thing.

"So, I haven't asked you yet," Wyatt said as he hung up the girls' snow pants, "but you seem to know your way around equipment and cows. How is that?"

Adele picked up Maria's wet toque and mitts, laying them out on the bench to dry. "I spent a lot of time on a farm."

"So, you grew up on one?"

"Sort of." Adele gave a shrug, then looked at him, her expression unreadable. "My foster parents had a farm. They took care of me when my dad...when my dad couldn't. I helped them out whenever I was there."

She sounded casual, but despite his own weak state, Wyatt sensed a tension as she spoke.

"How big was their place?" he asked, avoiding the topic of why her father couldn't take care of her. Sensing she would prefer to stick to basic facts.

"It wasn't large. About a hundred cow/calf pairs. Earl, my foster father, sometimes kept steers back and grass-fed them."

"Where was this ranch?"

"In Fairview. But up there, it was never called a ranch," she said with a quick smile, hanging her own coat up. "People up there don't stand on ceremony. My foster parents always called it a farm. Plain and simple."

He had to smile at her comment. "Well, my place is a ranch. Always has been a ranch, always will be."

He stood aside to let her precede him into the kitchen. He followed her and grabbed the kettle, filling it with water. "Do you want some coffee? Tea? I was going to make some hot chocolate for the kids."

"I'll have some of the same," she said, hovering in the middle of the kitchen, as if unsure what to do.

"Cocoa is on the shelf above the stove." He plugged the kettle in. He pulled some mugs out of the cupboard and spoons out of the drawer just as Adele handed him the cocoa. "Marshmallows are in the pantry."

Adele shot him a curious look. "You have a pantry? That would have been good to know when I was scrounging through the cupboards looking for something to make last night. Or when I was putting away the groceries just now."

"It's behind me. The door beside the one leading to my office."

"And here I thought I'd be snooping if I opened it." Adele chuckled as she walked over and opened the correct door. Then she sighed. "Well, this isn't exactly Mother Hubbard's cupboard, but it comes close."

"Sorry. Cooking is not my superpower," he said, spooning powder into the mugs he had set out.

"I can see that. The freezer and refrigerator were pretty bare too."

He leaned back against the counter, fighting another wave of weakness. "Were pretty bare?" he repeated, turning it into a question.

"I got groceries when I went to town."

Guilt washed over him. "I'm so sorry. I should pay you back for that."

"Just add it to my paycheck," she said with a grin. "As for the marshmallows, I'm thinking they've celebrated a few birthdays already." The bag made a thunk when she dropped it on the counter.

"Oh well, I tried."

She tossed the bag into the garbage can beside the counters. "I'm sure you did more than that," she said, her voice quiet. "It's quite a responsibility to manage a ranch and raise two little girls."

"It's been a challenge, is all I can say."

"I'm sure it has been." She was quiet a moment. He felt her eyes on him and he wondered what she was thinking.

"How many years has it been since you've lived on the ranch—I mean farm?" he asked, unwilling to stop their conversation. He felt like it had been ages since he'd talked with an adult in an adult manner. Ruby wasn't one for chit-chat and he never encouraged it.

"I left when I was eighteen. The usual country kid story. Couldn't wait to get to the big city."

"But I thought you said you lived in Whitehorse?"

"Which is big compared to Fairview," she countered. "I ended up there following some guy I thought would give me a happy ever after."

"I take it he didn't?" Wyatt poured the hot water into the mugs, shooting her a quick glance.

She was smiling. "No. I found out that only happens in Hallmark movies. Which I love, by the way."

"You don't need to defend them to me. I've watched a few from time to time. Gets pretty quiet in the evenings when the girls are in bed." And didn't that make him sound like a total loser?

"It's light and comfortable entertainment. I have to confess,

75

I'm always sad when Christmas is over. I love a good Christmas romance."

He laughed at that, wondering about her romantic history. A woman as attractive as she was had to have had at least one boyfriend, besides the man she followed to Whitehorse. But he knew it would be inappropriate to ask.

Just then Dean wandered into the kitchen. He walked over to Adele and leaned against her, looking over at Wyatt, his expression serious.

"What's up, buddy?" she asked, fingering his hair back from his eyes.

But Dean didn't turn his intent gaze from Wyatt.

"So, are you really my daddy?" he asked, uncertainty tingeing his voice.

The question was like a gut punch. There was no way to answer it without either raising false hopes or looking like a heel. Wyatt shot a panicked glance to Adele, but she was looking down at Dean, her lips pressed together as if holding her emotions in check.

Once again frustration surged through him. How could the boy's mother have done this to him? How could she have planted this false hope? He thought of the DNA test now, hopefully, winging its way to Calgary. Exonerating him.

"I think you're a nice boy," was all Wyatt dared say, struggling to find the right words. Until he knew for sure, he hardly dared raise the little guy's hopes.

Dean laid his head against Adele, who had slipped her arm around him. "I miss my mommy," he said, his voice trembling.

Wyatt felt horrible. But what could he do? What could he say?

Tears slipped down Dean's cheeks and he swiped at his nose. Adele reached over and grabbed a tissue from a box that hadn't been there before she had come. She'd thought of everything. She knelt down beside Dean, wiped his eyes, and handed the

Kleenex to him for him to blow his nose. She gave him a tender hug, stroking his back.

"Honey, right now we have to wait for some...some stuff to come back. Some important papers." She bit her lip again, as if she knew her answer created more questions.

Dean sniffed again and Adele gave him another hug.

Watching her, Wyatt felt a shaft of bitter anger toward Theresa. Adele had more affection for a child that wasn't hers than Theresa had for her own biological daughters.

He knew Adele was here to bring Dean to him, but from the way she was interacting with the little guy, in the sympathetic glisten of moisture in her eyes, she wouldn't be able to walk away so easily. The thought gave some hope for the little boy's future.

"My mommy said he'd be happy to see me," Dean sniffed, wiping his nose again. He looked up at Adele in question, as if looking for an answer from her.

"Oh, honey," Adele said, her voice breaking.

Wyatt could tell she was struggling, and he wished he could help her out.

Wyatt watched Dean, wishing, praying he could remember. But his brain was still fuzzy from the flu, and he was tired.

But Dean's sorrow caught at his heart, and before he could tell himself otherwise, he got up, walked over, and knelt down beside him. He laid his hand on Dean's shoulder, rubbing back and forth. "You're a sweet little boy," he said. "I'm sure your mother loved you very much."

Dean nodded, blinking as he stared at him.

As their eyes met, a memory trembled in the recesses of his brain, some sense of familiarity. Wyatt didn't know if he was projecting, but there was something about this little boy that looked familiar.

"We made you and the girls some hot chocolate," Adele said, standing, her hand still on Dean's other shoulder. "Why don't you get Maya and Maria and ask them to come into the kitchen. You can drink it here at the table with us and have some of those cookies I promised."

Dean blinked back tears, but thankfully, he left to go get the girls.

As he did, Adele shot Wyatt a questioning glance, as if hoping for some answer from him.

But all he could give her was a vague shrug. The girls burst into the kitchen and spared him having to say anything more.

He set the mugs out and some spoons then sat down himself, and a few moments later, they were all sitting together around the table.

Wyatt felt a flitter of sorrow. Here he was, sitting at the table with a complete stranger and three little kids, like a small family. He shot a glance at Adele and caught the melancholy look on her face. He wondered if she was thinking the same thing.

"We watched a good show," Maya said. "My brain is still good."

"Glad to hear that," Wyatt said with a chuckle. He glanced over at Adele, who was frowning. "I always tell the girls that if they watch too much TV their brains will stop working."

Adele chuckled. "That's funny, Sally always said the same thing to Dean."

Again, that tremor of uncertainty as he tried to recall that trip.

"I think we should play a game together," Adele said to Maya. "We want your brain to keep working."

"We can play the bear game," Maria announced, jumping off her chair and licking the hot cocoa mustache off her lip. She scooted away and returned with a large box and dropped it on the table with a rattle.

"But you can only play with four people," Wyatt said.

"Me and my dad together," Maria announced. And that was that.

"He's my dad too," Maya said with a touch of asperity.

"I'm a dad to both of you," Wyatt said with a shake of his head. The girls could be fiercely competitive. Just then he caught Dean looking at him and sensed the question in his eyes.

He looked away, handing Maya the dice.

She shook them and tossed them on the board with a cheer. And the game was on. They sent the characters along the board, sometimes going backwards when they got a sad card, sometimes going ahead when they grabbed a happy card. Wyatt read the cards out loud, and Dean got into the game, excited when he jumped ahead.

As they played, Wyatt couldn't keep his eyes off the boy. Something about him struck a memory.

Once again Wyatt was surprised at how easily the girls accepted Dean's presence. He couldn't figure that one out. But he put it down to the fact that the girls spent a lot time on their own. They were probably happy to have a friend.

A few more rolls of the dice and the game was over. Dean, to the girl's chagrin, had won. He was beaming and Maya was pouting. "Be a good sport," Wyatt warned his daughter. She wrinkled her nose at him then looked over at Dean. "You played a good game," she said, imitating her Uncle Reuben's usual reply whenever he played with them.

Adele smiled at that, getting to her feet. "I have to get some supper ready," she said, "if you want to play again."

"Nope. Don't want to lose again," Maya retorted. Then she looked over at Wyatt, who was about to reprimand her. "Sorry. Not a good sport."

"You got that right." He tweaked her nose then patted her head. "But we can play again after supper."

He stood then grabbed the back of the chair, wavering. He

caught Adele's concerned look, but he waved it off. "I'm fine," he said. "I should get some work done in the shop."

"What time do you want to eat?" she asked.

"About six o'clock? Does that work for you?"

"That would work just fine," Adele said.

Goodness, they sounded like some married couple.

As he walked to the porch to get dressed again, he pushed the thought aside. He was being ridiculous. She was a nanny, he reminded himself. He didn't want to think about how long it would last, but for now at least peace was reigning in his house, peace they hadn't experienced in a long time. No need to complicate it.

Adele wiped down the counters and glanced over at Dean.

He sat at the table, making a tiny log house out of the toothpicks he'd found in a container on the table.

"I think we better get going," she said to him. It was still early but Wyatt was putting the twins to bed. She could leave.

He shook his head. "I'm not tired yet."

She knew she should press the issue but she wasn't keen on making the drive in the dark just yet. Besides, once Wyatt had the girls in bed, it would give him some time to be with Dean. Get to know him.

"I know there's some books on the bookshelf. I'll read you some stories," she said. "But once we're done, then it's time to go."

Dean nodded and cleaned up the toothpicks without being asked. Adele helped him and then together they went into the family room.

Adele felt once again a sense of unreality. They were here in a stranger's house yet she felt completely at home. *Wishful thinking,* she said to herself. Trying to replace the home she had lost when Earl died.

She shook off the silly thought and walked over to the bookshelf to find the books she'd discovered the other day.

Dean cuddled up beside her as she opened one of the books and started to read. The ease with which he snuggled up to her created another unwelcome pang. How could she leave him here?

And once again, she felt a shiver of anger with her friend for keeping Dean away from his father this long. For not letting Dean know earlier who he was.

She forced her mind back to the story about a fire engine that wanted adventure. The book was written in rhyme, and Adele caught the soothing cadence of the book, getting pulled into the story. Dean leaned forward, looking at the pictures, smiling with each adventure the fire engine got into. He laughed in a few places.

As she turned the last page, Wyatt came down the stairs. He paused at the bottom, looking at them both with a quizzical expression on his face. Maybe he was thinking the same thing she was. How did they all end up here?

"My mom read those books to me and my brothers," he said, dropping onto the couch opposite her.

"I figured they were older books," Adele said, running her finger over a pencil doodle that someone had added to one page. "They look well read."

"It's one of a set that we got from a lady in the church, Dot Westerveld. She was on a one-woman mission to make the young population of Millars Crossing literate. She would give books out at Christmas at church."

"A book is the gift that keeps on giving," Adele said with a smile.

She caught Wyatt's eyes on hers and once again had a hard time looking away.

She forced her attention back to the book she was reading, but the entire time she read, she felt Wyatt's attention on her and Dean. It unsettled and fascinated her.

A few books later, she glanced up at the clock. "Okay, buddy, we need to get going."

Dean stretched, then stood, glancing over at Wyatt. For a moment Adele thought he would ask him another awkward question. Instead he just gave Wyatt a careful smile.

"Goodnight...Mr. Wy-Wyatt," he said, stumbling over the name.

Wyatt stood. "Good night, kiddo," he said, reaching out and ruffling Dean's hair.

Adele swallowed at the sight. Was Wyatt coming to grips with the fact of his fatherhood? Or was he just being nice?

Dean walked away and Adele looked at Wyatt. "Thanks for the kindness," she said, wanting to acknowledge the tentative gesture he had given Dean.

"He's a good kid," he said, adding a shrug, as if his admission was dragged out of him.

"He is. He's a real sweetheart."

Wyatt pressed his lips together and Adele guessed she had pushed things too far. Campaigned maybe a bit too hard.

"What time do you want me to come tomorrow?" she asked.

"Whatever works for you. I need to bring my snow machine into town tomorrow for some repairs, but I don't need to leave until about ten."

"I can come for breakfast."

"You don't need to do that," he protested, but Adele sensed he was being polite.

"I don't mind. I have little else to do." She smiled at him and she could see a tension in his shoulders release.

"Okay. That'd be great."

As they stood across from each other, Adele felt something else slip into the atmosphere. A sense of waiting, expectation.

Was it just her imagination, or did Wyatt move just a little closer to her? Did his features soften just a little as their gazes held?

She was being silly. She spun away, breaking the connection.

But he followed her to the entrance, putting his own coat and boots on as she helped Dean struggle into his snow pants.

"Where's your keys?" he asked, zipping up his parka. "I'll start your car."

Adele could only stare at him, surprised at the offer. Then she pulled herself together and grabbed her purse, unzipping it. "Thanks so much. That's very kind."

"Just common sense," he said, taking them from her. Their hands brushed each other, a faint tingle dancing up her fingers to her chest. "It's cold out. Your car should warm up a bit." His brusque tone seemed to negate the kindness of his offer, but the faint smile he gave her balanced that out.

Then without another word, he stepped outside.

Adele felt a flicker of warmth at the chivalrous offer. Earl used to start her car for her as well. It had been years since anyone had been so thoughtful. It was a small thing, but it made her feel cared for.

Again, she reminded herself that he was just being polite. Reminded herself to be careful. She got Dean's mittens on and his boots tied when Wyatt returned, brushing some snow off his coat. "Be cautious out there. It's snowing, and your visibility won't be great. We get deer wandering the roads in the night. You won't want to hit one of them with that little car."

"I will be, thanks again," she said, slipping on her own coat.

She slung her purse over her shoulder and gave him another look. But his eyes were on Dean, as if still trying to puzzle out where he fit into his life.

The snow was falling gently now, illuminated by the light shining from the roof of the entrance. The snow hadn't collected too much, so they easily made their way to the car, following the steps Wyatt had made. He had brushed some of the gathering snow off her windshield so she didn't have to do that either.

As she got in she shot one more look back to the house, surprised to see Wyatt framed in the doorway, his arms crossed, watching her.

Again, that feeling of being cared for washed over her. She helped Dean into the car then got in herself.

With a quick wave to Wyatt, she backed up, then drove carefully all the way back to town.

The snow had quit by the time she got back to the place she was staying. A chilly wind swirled around them though, and Adele hoped the weather wouldn't turn bad. It would make the drive to the ranch difficult tomorrow.

"It's straight to bed, okay?" she told Dean as she set her purse on the bench just inside the house.

He didn't protest and a few minutes later she was supervising him brushing his teeth then tucking him in bed.

The whole time she got him ready, she had the sense of unreality. Taking care of this little boy was growing more dangerous by the moment. Yes, she had lived with him and Sally, but Sally had always done most of the work. Sometimes Adele pitched in, but mostly she kept her distance. Sally preferred it that way.

But now, the more time she spent with Dean, the more the little guy's presence hooked into her heart.

She knelt down beside the bed, stroking her hand over his face.

"So, tell me two good things about today," she said, remembering the little tradition Bonnie used to do with her each night.

"Sliding on the snow pile," Dean said, lacing his fingers together over his chest. "That was a lot of fun. I wish though we could have gotten another ride in the tractor."

"Well, that was just a one-off," Adele told him with a smile. "What's another thing?"

"Hot chocolate and playing that game," he said. His smile was replaced by a slight frown. "Is Mr. Wyatt really my daddy?"

Again, that concern. That question that shivered through her soul. How to reply to that?

"What makes you wonder?"

"He doesn't seem excited to see me. My mommy said he would be happy, but he seems kind of sad."

"He's not been feeling very good," was all Adele could manage.

Dean nodded, as if accepting this.

"We should pray now," he said instead.

Thanks to Dean, Adele had been praying a whole lot more in the last two days than she had in the last few years.

But a gentle yearning nudged her to take Dean's hands in hers, bow her head.

Dean recited the prayer that Adele remembered Sally praying with him each night. The words created another quiver of sorrow. And behind that came the feeling of frustration with her friend for creating false hopes in Dean.

"And thanks for letting me be with my...with Mr. Wyatt," Dean amended, his small correction creating another quiver. "I hope he gets better soon."

Adele laid her head on their joined hands, sending up her own prayer for strength and release of her concerns.

"Are you praying too?" Dean's small voice broke into her thoughts.

Adele kept her head there a moment, then looked up at him, smiling. "Just a little bit."

This seemed to satisfy him. She brushed a kiss over his forehead, got to her feet, and then left the room. She closed the door behind her and leaned against it, sending up yet another prayer. This one was formless, shapeless. Just a releasing of all the worries and concerns that dogged her. The unknown that hung over this poor, innocent little boy. As her foster mother would say, she laid everything in the large, strong hands of God.

He can carry your burdens better than you can, Bonnie used to tell her.

She pulled in a slow breath, feeling a surprising and unexpected sense of peace.

Maybe prayers work, she thought, pushing herself away from the door.

But as soon as she stepped into the living room, she realized she had left her backpack at the ranch. She felt lost without it.

She tried watching television but couldn't find anything that interested her. So she gave up and went to bed herself. But as she lay in the room, staring through the dark at the ceiling, her thoughts centered on Wyatt.

On how he watched her as she drove away.

CHAPTER SEVEN

"Go to church today, go to church today," Maya sang, brandishing her crayons as she colored the picture Adele had printed off for her and Maria.

She looked up at Adele, who was frying French toast for breakfast. "You come too." Her words were more of a command than a question, typical for the child.

"Yes, I come too," she said, wishing she could sound more enthusiastic about it.

"Church is fun," Maria put in, frowning as if sensing Adele's reluctance.

"I'm sure it can be."

It had been years since Adele attended, and the only reason she was going today was for Dean. Sally took him all the time and if Wyatt and his daughters went, then Dean should too.

She glanced at the clock again, wondering when Wyatt would return.

The past few days Adele, Dean, the girls, and Wyatt had slipped into an easy rhythm. Adele and Dean always arrived before the twins got up, netting some grumbling from Dean about how the girls got to sleep in but he didn't. She made breakfast each morning, which they all ate together, and then Wyatt left to feed and bed the cows and get some work done in his shop that he said had been waiting for weeks. While he came in for lunch, he often grabbed a quick sandwich then left. She usually made supper for the family. They would eat together and then she and Dean would leave for town.

Apparently, the previous nanny wasn't very reliable and Wyatt didn't dare leave her alone with the kids too long. So he had been falling behind on maintenance of the tractor and a bunch of welding and repairs on other pieces of equipment that kept him busy.

Yesterday it was the hay bine that he'd been struggling to find the time to repair since the last time he used it in the fall.

She looked up at the clock, wondering if she should send him a text that breakfast was ready. They had to eat, and she had to clean up the girls and get them ready for church—all within the next hour.

"I'm hungry," Maria announced, looking up from her picture. "Can we eat now?"

Adele agreed, but hoped Wyatt would come back on time. She knew he didn't enjoy missing meals with the girls.

She cleared off the table with the help of the kids, and got the plates and utensils on the table. Adele waited, listening, but Wyatt wasn't back at the house yet. So she pulled out her phone and sent him a quick text, hoping he hadn't hurt himself. Hoped he was okay.

He's fine. Stop worrying.

Adele shook off her concerns. But as she set the plate of French toast on the table beside the sausages she had fried, she couldn't stop her mind from ticking back to another fateful Sunday. When her foster father had been out feeding the cows. He was late coming in, so Bonnie headed out to see what was taking him so long. She came running back to the house, calling out for Adele to call 911, then ran out again.

Adele had done so then ran out to join Bonnie. She found her kneeling beside Earl, who was pinned between a bale and the forks, praying, praying, too frightened to cry. He was still alive when the ambulance came.

Bonnie went with him in the ambulance, leaving Adele to move the tractor back into the barn.

And wait.

Two hours later someone from the church got her and took her to the hospital.

Earl Stefanski died that night.

She shook off the horrible memory, pushing it way down. That was years ago, and she wasn't that frightened young girl anymore, begging God to do the impossible.

Then her phone beeped. It was Wyatt. He was coming up in a few minutes. *Start without me*, he texted.

She was surprised at the flush of relief washing through her.

"We pray," Maya announced, as they all sat down.

They looked to her, expecting her to do the honors. "Umm, we can wait for your dad."

"You can pray," Maya said, frowning at her.

Adele knew it wasn't worth arguing with the girl. Once Maya set her mind to something, it either happened, or you started something you quickly wish you hadn't.

Okay. *Here goes.* She bowed her head and took Dean and Maria's hands in hers. "Thank you, Lord, for the food. Thank you for Sunday. Help us to be good. Amen."

She looked up to catch Maya frowning at her. "That was short."

Adele hadn't expected a critique of her prayer and, despite the disapproval Maya was telegraphing, she had to smile. "Did you want to pray?" she asked.

"Nope. Already done."

Adele chuckled. Maya was worming her precocious way into Adele's heart. Along with Maria.

And Wyatt?

"Then let's eat."

They were just about finished when the back door opened and Wyatt stepped inside.

And just like that, Adele's heart did a silly little jump. She tried to keep her attention on the kids, but as soon as he came into the kitchen, her eyes leaped to his. And, to her dismay, he was watching her.

"We...we started without you," she said, startled at the breathless tone of her voice.

"I see that," he returned, smiling.

"It's good, Daddy," Maria called out. "You sit here." She patted the empty spot beside her.

"Just let me wash up and I'll be right back."

And as he passed her, Adele caught a whiff of cool outdoor air, hay, and the faintest scent of diesel.

Masculine and appealing.

He came back a few moments later. He had put on another shirt, a beige twill one, tucked into clean blue jeans. As he sat down, his eyes ticked over the girls, stopping on Dean, as if still trying to figure out who he was.

"This looks great, doesn't it, girls?" he said with a note of appreciation as he glanced over at Adele. Once again, for the tiniest of moments, their eyes held a fraction longer than necessary.

Once again, that unwelcome trill shivered down her spine.

That DNA test can't come fast enough, Adele thought.

"It delicious," Maria said, pushing a plate toward him. "You need sausages too."

"Thanks, sweetie," he said, stroking her hair, smiling down at her.

Wyatt's interactions with his daughters were so easy, so

unrehearsed. So casual and loving. It wasn't hard to see how much he loved the girls.

Adele glanced over at Dean, but he was wiping up the syrup on his plate with the last of his French toast. Would Wyatt be able to love Dean the same?

"Are you and Dean coming to church with us?" Wyatt asked, looking up from his breakfast to Adele, who had gotten up and poured him a cup of coffee.

"Yes. They are," Maya announced, jumping off her chair and standing by Dean, tugging on his arm. "Hurry. We need to play."

"Like Maya said, we are," Adele said, picking up the kids' plates, avoiding looking at him. "I know Sally attended with Dean, and though I only took him occasionally...I'd like...I think he should go."

"I have to agree."

Adele was thankful for his comment. The closest he had come to making any kind of commitment to Dean. She brought the plates to the sink, rinsed them, and stacked them in the dishwasher. He brought his over as well and dropped it onto a rack. He hesitated as if he wanted to say more. Adele glanced his way, once again their eyes meeting, holding. Once again that indefinable attraction humming between them.

It was as if time stopped, waiting for something to happen.

Adele pulled in a slow breath, telling herself to stop doing this. To stop encouraging this growing attraction.

Wyatt shifted, shook his head to break the connection, then left.

Adele's heart stuttered in her chest. Nothing had happened. Nothing at all, and yet she felt as if she and Wyatt were edging toward something she couldn't indulge in.

Adele stood, clinging to the pew in front of her as the pastor announced the last song.

"The blessing of a family, the family of God, carried through our weaknesses, stronger than blood," the congregation sang.

An unexpected sorrow wove through her heart, bringing back memories of sitting in church with her foster parents. She always sat between them, their arms over her shoulders, as if protecting her. She always felt safe and loved there.

Pulling in a deep breath, she gathered her emotions, pushing down the memories. The minister's sermon had been about community and family. His words had settled into her soul, and she was still trying to sort them all out. At one time she had a family, and then it all disappeared. She had prayed and prayed, but God hadn't been there.

She sent a glance at Wyatt only to find him looking at her again. This was happening too much, and she knew she had to put a stop to it. But the loneliness that had been dogging her the last few years kept her eyes locked on his.

Dean had wanted to go with the girls to Sunday school, so it was just her and Wyatt in the pew. When they'd walked into church together, she sensed people watching them. Though she shouldn't care, she wondered what they thought.

She dragged her gaze away, turning her attention to the front of the church.

The last chords of the song resounded through the church and Adele released a gentle sigh. She had made it through the service without falling into the emotions that threatened to choke her.

She slipped her purse over her shoulder, folding her arms over her stomach, glancing around, trying to figure out how to leave.

"We can go out here," Wyatt said, pointing to a side door only a few feet away.

Adele nodded, waiting as the people beside her made their way out into the aisle.

Just as she was about to go through the door someone called her name.

Frowning, she stopped and turned to see Mrs. Flikkema waving at her, working her way through the gathering crowd of people trying to leave.

"I'll get the kids if you need to talk to her," Wyatt said.

Adele nodded, stepping aside to let the other people pass her.

"I'm so glad I caught you. I was trying to call your cell phone this morning," Mrs. Flikkema said, breathless, her face pink. She looked flustered. "I know this is an imposition and I apologize, but I'm stuck. My daughter and her husband have to come to Millars Crossing. My son-in-law's father isn't doing well and they want to see him." Mrs. Flikkema paused, taking in another breath, and Adele waited, wondering why she was telling her this. "So, here's my dilemma. They can't stay with his parents. The house is full. And I don't want them to stay in a hotel. So I was wondering, seeing as how you're mostly at the ranch anyhow, if they could stay in the suite tonight, maybe tomorrow night."

As her words sank in, Adele realized what she was asking. She hesitated, wondering what she should do.

"I know it's a lot to ask, and it leaves you in a bit of a lurch..." She paused and pulled Adele farther away from the last of the people leaving the church. She moved closer, lowering her voice. "I phoned the Millars Crossing Inn. They have an empty room. I would gladly pay for it."

"Okay. I could do that." When she had first planned her trip to Millars Crossing, Adele had looked at staying at the Inn, but she wasn't sure how things would go at the ranch and didn't want to spend her time sitting with Dean in a hotel room. The basement suite at Angie Flikkema's place was much more appealing.

"Thanks so much. I appreciate this."

"I'll come by after church to pick up my things," Adele said.

Mrs. Flikkema almost sagged in relief. "I'm so sorry about all of this, and I know it's a huge ask, but it would make things so much easier for my daughter and her husband. They're already dealing with a lot of stress."

"Don't worry. It'll be fine," Adele assured her.

Mrs. Flikkema caught her hand and squeezed it. "Thank you. You are such a good person. I'll see you later."

Adele nodded, then zipped up her coat, looking for the exits.

"We're here," Maya cried out, bursting through the door ahead of her, holding on to what looked like a tree with some ragged paper leaves attached to it. "We can go now."

Dean lagged behind them, looking down at a paper he was holding. Wyatt was right behind them, holding Maria's hand.

"What did Angie Flikkema want?" he asked as they joined her.

"She needs the Airbnb for her daughter."

"That means you'll need another place to stay."

"She called the Inn. There's a room available Dean and I can stay in. We'll have to go pick up our stuff."

Wyatt nodded slowly. "You can't check in until four o'clock, so we'll just get your stuff to the ranch for now. We'll have to make a couple of stops on the way."

"A couple?" she asked as they walked to the truck, pulling the hood of her coat against the bitter wind.

"I need to check the mail," he said.

The words came out casually but Adele comprehended the import in them. She had gone to town on Friday but hadn't taken the key for the mailbox along, so they hadn't picked up the mail for a few days.

Maybe. Maybe.

They walked to the truck and got in. The girls were chattering about the Sunday school class.

"What did you learn?" Adele asked Dean, who was quiet.

"We talked about family," he mumbled, looking down.

Adele guessed that the theme of the church service was echoed downstairs. A theme that it seemed both she and Dean struggled with.

She left it at that, turning to look through the windshield at the snow now swirling around.

They drove directly to the Airbnb, and while Wyatt waited in the truck with the kids, Adele went inside and made quick work of gathering what few items they had left. It didn't take long, and a few minutes later she was trundling their suitcases down the snow-covered walk.

Wyatt got out of the truck and helped her lift them into the bed of the truck. As he did, their hands brushed each other and once again that unwelcome electricity sprang between them.

Their next stop was the mailbox, and this time Adele stayed behind as Wyatt got out and went to the bank of mailboxes on the side of the road. He fumbled with the key, shrugging up his shoulders against the blowing snow. Adele hoped it wouldn't snow too much. She had to get out tonight, and her car didn't have the clearance that Wyatt's truck did.

He returned with a stack of envelopes and Adele felt a shiver of apprehension as he got into the truck. He lifted the lid of the console between them and dropped them inside. Then he looked over at her and nodded. She guessed that meant the results were back.

She swallowed, pulling in a deep breath. Then, again, she sent up a formless prayer to the God she had been avoiding so long. A God whose hand had brushed her soul this morning, reminding her that at one time they had been close.

Trouble was, she wasn't sure what to pray for.

"I'll bring you back to town later this afternoon so you can get settled in the Inn," he said as he turned the truck around and then drove away, heading away from town.

Though the girls were chattering away, the drive back to the ranch was tense, and Adele guessed Wyatt was dealing with the same stress she was. Probably more. The envelope seemed to radiate an energy.

And the Oscar goes to...

When they got back, the kids tumbled out of the vehicle, Adele and Wyatt trailing behind them.

Once inside, Adele heated up the soup she had made the day before and put out some buns. Again, the bulk of the conversation was taken up by the girls talking about the Sunday school lesson.

"I'm finished," Maria announced, pushing her half-finished bowl of soup away. "Can we watch television?" She angled a sly smile Adele's way.

She was about to say an automatic no when Wyatt got up.

"I'll put on a DVD for you," he said, giving in.

Dean, Maya, and Maria all scrambled off their chairs, hurrying to the family room behind Wyatt.

Adele cradled her coffee, staring at the envelopes stacked on one end of the counter. She knew she should start cleaning up, but needed a moment to gather her thoughts.

Ever since she sat down in church, she'd felt as if she were on an emotional roller coaster. The service had hit her harder than she thought possible. The memories of sitting with Bonnie and Earl Stefanski had invaded her mind, stolen her peace. And yet, despite that, she had also glimpsed the promises of contentment and joy she had felt from that time. She may have tried to avoid God, but it seemed He was still looking for her and using whatever circumstances He could to draw her near.

Wyatt came back, slid the door between the two rooms closed, and without a word walked over to the mail. He returned with one envelope, set it on the table, and dropped into his chair.

"Well, I guess this is it," he said, picking it up.

Adele clung to her mug, pulling in a breath to steady the pounding of her heart.

He ripped it open, his movements unsteady, and then he dragged the paper out. He held it a moment, looking from it to Adele as if unsure how to proceed. Then he opened it, pulling out a sheaf of papers. His eyes flicked over the first page. He blinked and read it again. Shuffled the other papers, skimmed over them.

Adele strained to read his expression.

Then, finally, he looked over at her, leaning back in his chair, still holding the paper.

"Well. According to this, Dean is my son."

CHAPTER EIGHT

*W*yatt read the papers again and again, feeling as if the ground had been swept out from under him.

"You're sure?" Adele asked, her voice as shaky as he was feeling.

"They say the results are ninety-nine point and a bunch of nines accurate," Wyatt said, holding the papers with trembling hands, still trying to absorb their contents. "That's a solid result."

"Now we know."

Wyatt still wasn't sure what to make of this. Still wasn't sure how to feel. He folded the papers and tried to slip them into the envelope. His movements were awkward, jerky. He got them inside and then leaned back in his chair, trying to catch his balance and his breath.

His heart was jumping around in his chest like a kangaroo, and he didn't know which emotion to grab on to. Which emotion was legitimate.

Confusion. Fear. Concern.

How could he not remember the mother of his son? What

kind of person did that make him?

"Can you show me that picture of Sally again?" he asked, struggling to make sense of the situation. He had been so positive that Dean wasn't his child.

But I can see glimpses of my family in him, he thought as Adele pulled out her phone and flicked her fingers over the screen.

She found the picture and handed him the phone. Wyatt looked at Sally again, trying to see her from a different perspective. He set the phone down and dragged his hands over his face, trying to settle his emotions. Thinking back to over five years ago. That trip to Mexico.

Then something occurred to him.

"I'll be right back," he told Adele. He remembered the photo book Reuben's wife, Denise, had made of their trip to Mexico. Maybe there would be something in there. Some picture.

He slid open the door to the family room.

"Not yet, Daddy," Maya called out, holding out her hands toward the television as if to stop whatever he might think of doing.

"Don't worry, honey," Wyatt assured her. "You can watch until it's over." *And maybe another one after that*, he thought, *the way things are going*. His gaze shifted to Dean, who was staring, riveted by the dancing cake on the screen in front of him. He had seen the boy all week but now, trying to see him as his son...

He felt a thickening in his throat and he swallowed it down. Sure, he was a good kid and a nice little boy...but his son?

Could he love him as much as he loved his daughters?

One step at time, he reminded himself.

Shaking off the emotions, he walked over to the bookshelf and, squatting down, pulled open a door of a cupboard below it. He hadn't gone in here in ages. He pulled out various photo albums, trying to make himself slow down and be deliberate. As he sorted through the books, he was acutely aware of the little boy sitting with his daughters.

His son.

Wyatt paused, holding on to the shelf in front of him, still feeling off balance. His entire world had shifted, tilted.

Please, Lord, was all he could pray.

He moved a few more albums aside, now wondering if he still had the book. Then he saw it, tucked way in the back, sitting sideways behind a couple of coffee table books that Theresa had purchased to make their home look more elegant.

He pulled the book out and stood, flipping quickly through it.

"Did you find anything?" Adele was right behind him, obviously also curious.

Not that he blamed her. She had a lot at stake as well.

"I'll take this into the kitchen," he said, closing the book and turning toward her.

Her smile looked strained and he could see a sadness deep in her eyes.

Had she hoped the test would come back negative?

He walked into the kitchen, glancing once again at Dean. This time the boy looked up at him and smiled.

The sight sent a hook into his heart. He paused, then returned his smile. Dean looked away, back at the television, the moment passed.

Wyatt closed the door again and dropped the book onto the table. "This is a photo album from that trip Reuben and I took," he said, sitting down again.

Adele pulled up a chair right beside him, tucking her hair behind her ear. He caught a whiff of her perfume and felt a tiny clench in his gut. She looked sad.

He brushed his reaction off and opened the book, paging through it, checking out each picture. In the middle there was a full-page spread of a group they had spent some time with.

"Is that you?" Adele asked, pointing.

Wyatt stared more closely at it, struggling with a surge of shame. "Yeah, that's me."

His hair was a disaster, his eyes bleary, and he was holding up a glass of something. Hard liquor, he presumed. He wasn't much of a beer drinker.

"Not my best moment," he muttered. "Reuben asked me to come on the trip with him because I had just broken up with Theresa. It was an ugly situation." He sighed, shaking his head.

"Ugly with Theresa?" Adele asked.

"Yeah. We were on again, off again. Like we couldn't make up our minds." He tried to erase that time out of his head. "Actually, more like I couldn't decide. I would break up with her and then she'd beg me to come back and, fool that I was, I fell for it every time."

"And then you married her."

"Yeah. Still not sure how I got suckered into that. We eloped. Her idea. I think she wanted to make sure I didn't get away a fourth time." Wyatt sighed and looked over the picture, trying to see something. Anything.

"Who is this?" Adele pointed to a young, thin girl, bright blue eyes, her long blonde hair falling over her shoulders. She was standing beside Wyatt, a faint smirk on her face, her arm tucked in his.

Wyatt leaned in closer, as if to see better. He sorted back through his memories. "Can't remember her name," he said. Then as he looked, a few vague memories returned. He stared, tugging at the thoughts that surfaced. "I think she told me her name was Jane?"

And then it all came crashing back. "I just met her that night. She came on to me in a big way. I tried to brush her off but she wouldn't leave me alone. I was lonely and drunk..." He faltered, the shame of that night coming back. Hard. "That was no excuse. I know that. But she came up to my room. I can't remember much,

I'm ashamed to say. But the next morning she was gone. I tried to find out where she was staying. Who she really was. I suspected Jane wasn't her real name, but I had no idea how to find her." He stopped, wondering why he felt the need to explain. Justify.

He knew it was because he didn't want Adele to think less of him. Wanted her to realize he wasn't the jerk the situation made him look like.

"You never found her?"

Wyatt shook his head, still looking at the book. "I didn't have a picture of her. Only a description. I spent the whole morning asking around. I talked to an employee at the resort who had just come on shift and remembered her from the night before. Jane wasn't staying at the resort, but he remembered her because she tipped him a lot of money. Apparently to keep me in drinks." He shook his head, still frustrated with how easily he'd been duped.

"Sounds like she had a plan to seduce you," Adele said softly.

Was that understanding he heard in her voice?

"Doesn't matter. I shouldn't have fallen for it." Wyatt glanced over the page again, the shameful memories returning.

Then Adele reached out for the book. "Can I have a look?"

Wyatt gave it to her, looking over at the sliding door. The kids were still watching the television.

His daughters.

And his son.

"You're sure this is the girl?" Adele asked, pointing to Jane.

Wyatt nodded.

"I think that's Sally. Thinner, blonder." Adele started typing on her phone. "I met Sally only a couple of years ago. She already had Dean," she said, sounding distracted. "But I am friends...was friends...with her on Facebook. I haven't deactivated her account yet. Her mother wanted me to keep it up for a while."

Biting her lip, she started flicking her finger, frowning at her screen, then stopped, nodding. She laid the phone on the table, turning it so he could see the screen. "Here. An older picture. From before I knew her."

The picture was, again, of a crowd of people. Adele enlarged the picture, zooming in on a girl. Same long blonde hair as Jane. Same sly smile. He put the photo book closer and then he saw the resemblance.

"That's her. That's Jane, or, as it might appear, Sally."

Adele ran her index finger back and forth over her lips as if thinking. "That certainly looks like her. And the timing would match up. I just wonder why she went under another name."

"For the record, she was the only girl I slept with before I married Theresa. Again, Wyatt felt the need to defend himself.

Adele looked from the phone to the book, frowning, as if thinking. "I think that was about the time she was separated from her husband. Sally always made it sound like Dean was her ex-husband Paul's kid. And she never mentioned a trip to Mexico. Nothing on her Facebook page about that either." Adele frowned then looked over at Wyatt, her eyes wide. "And Jane was her mother's name and Sally's middle name."

"Okay. That all adds up then." Wyatt blew out his breath, trying to find his balance in this new place. "I have a son."

Though he spoke quietly, the four words resonated through the kitchen, filling the space with the importance of their meaning.

Adele's head was lowered, her hair obscuring her features, but Wyatt saw the tears sliding down her cheeks. She swiped at them, pulling in a shaky breath.

The sight broke his heart, and he moved closer, slipping a comforting arm across her shoulders.

"I'm sorry. I know you brought him here with the idea of leaving, but I'm guessing this is hard for you too."

She nodded, fingering away another errant tear. "He's not my son, but I feel like he belongs to me in other ways."

Wyatt shifted a bit, pulling her closer, his heart breaking for her.

But behind the sorrow came another, deeper emotion. And when she lifted her face to his, when he looked deep into her shimmering eyes, sitting so close their breath tangled, he felt an inexorable pull toward her.

He wasn't sure who moved first but then their lips brushed, tentative, exploring. Her hand came to rest on his shoulder, then slipped around to the back of his neck, her fingers tangling in his hair.

And then their kiss deepened, altered.

Wyatt felt his heart thumping against his ribs, his feelings shifting, absorbing this amazing woman.

And then, reluctantly, other thoughts fed into the moment, growing more real, growing larger.

The kids.

She was leaving now.

He was the first to pull away and, to his surprise, she released a faint moan of protest, her hand tightening its grip on his neck. Then she too drew back.

But her eyes were fixed on his, as if trying to see him better.

"Please don't apologize," she whispered, lowering her hand to his shoulder but leaving it there.

He felt as if he should, but he also knew what she meant. Their kiss had shaken his foundation. Had sliced its way into his soul.

To apologize would trivialize and dismiss what he'd felt.

And from the flush on her cheeks and the glow in her eyes, he sensed she had been as moved as he.

"But now what?" he asked, unable to stop his hand from fingering a strand of hair away from her face. An excuse to touch her even though he knew he should stop.

She swallowed, her throat moving again, her teeth worrying her lower lip. "We keep our distance. I can't..." She let the words trail off then drew in a sigh. "I have my plans and I can't change them. I have to go to Edmonton for the auction. Then back to Whitehorse. Everything is in place."

Her bakery, he realized. Her own future.

As for his own situation, he was responsible for three children.

He pulled in a long breath, standing up, moving away from her so he wouldn't be tempted to touch her again.

"You're right. We have to keep our distance."

They were both silent as if trying to figure out how this would happen while she stayed to take care of the kids.

"You'll be going back to town tonight? Will you take Dean?"

Adele drew in a shuddering breath, then nodded. "I should. Maybe for tonight. Then tomorrow he can stay overnight here."

"And he already sees me as his father even though-" He stopped himself, guilt and confusion flowing through him.

"It will take time. I get that," Adele said, turning in her chair, giving him a smile of encouragement. "But you're a good father and a good man. I know you'll make this work."

"Thanks for the vote of confidence," he said with a short laugh. "I'm feeling overwhelmed right now."

She was quiet a moment, acknowledging his situation.

"Why don't we spend some time with the kids?" she asked. "Play a game with them? Read them some books?"

"Sounds like a good idea." He shoved his hand through his hair, then straightened his shoulders. "Just do what comes next," he said.

"That's what my foster father used to say."

Again, that oblique reference to her past that only whetted his curiosity about her.

But as he followed her into the family room where the kids were, he realized he might never find out. She wouldn't be sticking around long enough.

The thought created an unwelcome anxiety that twisted his

stomach with regret and lost chances.

Then, when he stepped into the room and saw Dean, he put his own feelings aside and gave his son a smile of encouragement.

"I win, I win." Maya jumped off her chair, spinning in a circle, her curls bouncing on her shoulders.

"You did," Wyatt agreed, "but I don't think you should celebrate so much."

Maya twisted her mouth, wrinkling her nose as if considering this. "But I win," she repeated, as if this made her victory dance even more valid.

Maria yawned, rubbing her eyes, and Adele shot a glance at the clock. Too early for bed and too late for a nap. "Should I make supper?" she asked, glancing over at Wyatt.

He looked at the clock as well, pushing his chair away from the table. "Might not be a bad idea. But I should check on the cows first. Make sure they're not bunched up in this storm."

As if to underline his comment, the wind gusted again, tossing snow against the windows. It had been storming all day and Adele had checked on the amount gathering on the deck every hour. She wanted to leave soon, but now that she knew for sure Dean was Wyatt's son, she wanted them to spend as much time together as possible.

While she was happy for Dean that they had settled his situation, it was still a wrench to realize her time with him was ending.

And with that, she relived the kiss she and Wyatt had shared a few hours ago. A kiss that felt as if it still warmed her lips, made her cheeks flush at the memory.

What had she been thinking?

Trouble was, she hadn't been.

And now she was torn between letting Dean be here as much as possible, knowing she promised Wyatt she would help him take care of the girls, and needing to leave for her own self-protection.

As Wyatt got up, his gaze slipped to hers, and despite her self-talk, she couldn't help the thrum of attraction that unsettled her heart. The arc of awareness that so easily sprang up between them. It had been building for days and now, after their kiss the flimsy barriers she was trying to erect again were torn down with just a look.

"I'll feed the kids and get the girls in bed," she said, forcing her attention back to the children. "Then Dean and I should leave."

She didn't catch Wyatt's reaction, nor was she checking to see it.

She busied herself with cleaning up the game, instructing the children to help.

She pulled out the leftover pizza from the day before, thankful that she had enough for today. It would make feeding the children quicker. Which meant she could leave sooner.

"I love pizza," Maya said, pulling a chair up to the counter as if to help. "You like pizza, Dean?"

"Not as much as hamburgers," Dean said.

"I like hamburgers," Maria announced, tucking her arm into Dean's. She stared up at him with a look of utter adoration.

Again, Adele was happy to see how quickly the children made a connection. As if they knew they were related.

She knew there would be a difficult time ahead for Dean after she left. She didn't want to think about that. That would make leaving too difficult.

And what about Wyatt?

She pushed that thought back down too, as she put the pizza on a cookie sheet and set it in the oven.

She got the kids to help her set the table as the pizza heated up, waiting for Wyatt to return.

Ten minutes later and he still wasn't back. She walked to the window, looking out. The swirling snow clouded her view. Would she even be able to get out of here?

Was Wyatt okay?

She turned back to the table, picked up the picture book, and brought it back to the family room, telling the kids to join her.

As she read them a story, Dean, Maya, and Maria snuggled up beside her. She struggled to keep her focus on the story, and not on how good it felt to be bracketed by the small warm bodies.

Finally, the door opened, and she heard Wyatt stomping the snow off his boots.

"Okay, kiddos," she said, closing the book and setting it aside. "We need to eat. And then Dean and I need to leave."

"I wish we could stay overnight," Dean said. "I don't want to go to an Inn."

"It'll be fun," Adele said, trying to inject a note of enthusiasm into her voice as she led the kids into the kitchen.

"I don't think so," Dean grumbled, looking over at Wyatt, who stood in the doorway. Then he grinned. "You look like a snowman."

Snow crusted Wyatt's hat and dusted his shoulders. Adele frowned at him, wondering why he wasn't coming in.

"Supper's ready," she said.

"Yeah, sure." He pulled his hat off, shook the snow off his coat, and hung it up.

He came inside the house, brushing remnants of snow from his hair. "It's nasty out there," he said with a note of concern. "I don't think your car will make it out of the driveway. In fact, I don't even think my truck will. I checked the forecast and there's a severe snowfall warning for the area. I'm sure the roads won't be graded."

"Are you saying I can't get out?"

"That's exactly what I'm saying. I think we're snowed in. And from the looks of the forecast, this storm will be around for a few days."

Adele stared at him as his words sank in. "So I'm not going anywhere?"

"I doubt it."

"Can we stay here tonight?" Dean asked, his tone hopeful.

"I think that's what will happen," Adele said. She was thankful they at least had their suitcases. But she hoped she wouldn't have to stay more than one night. The last time she'd stayed, Wyatt had been ill and in bed.

Now?

She shook the question off, determined to be practical. Determined to keep her heart whole. There would be no more kissing.

The timer on the oven dinged, and she pulled the pizza out. She made quick work of cutting it up and setting it out on the kids' plates. When they sat down, Dean ended up beside Wyatt. Adele wondered if he had set it up that way on purpose. When it was time to say grace, Wyatt held his hand out to Dean on one side and Maria on the other. It was what they did every supper-time, but somehow now, with all doubts about Dean's relation-ship to Wyatt erased, the moment felt even more poignant.

As if sensing where her thoughts were, Wyatt's glance grazed hers, and his gentle smile dove into her heart.

She bit her lip and lowered her head for him to pray. While he thanked God for the food and for safety, she added her own prayer.

Prayer for protection over her heart.

She knew far too well that love was like a cozy blanket. Comfortable and soft, but something that could get yanked away at any time. And when that happened—and it would—she knew she would be colder than she was before.

Better to keep herself aloof and safe.

CHAPTER NINE

"I'm glad we're staying here tonight," Dean said, snuggling into the bed he'd slept in before. "I like it at the ranch. And I like my daddy."

His words were like a hook in her heart. But they gave her a flicker of encouragement. He seemed to easily accept the situation he had been dropped in. Had quickly adjusted to being in this new place with his...yes...his sisters.

And his father.

All of this should make it easier for her when she left.

Then why didn't she feel happier?

She brushed his hair away from his face and pressed a gentle kiss to his forehead. "I think he likes you too."

Dean stared past Adele, his hands folded over his chest. "Why didn't I see my daddy before now?"

Adele was surprised this question hadn't come out sooner. But the poor kid had so many things dumped on him the past month he was probably still playing catch up. And now Adele had to think fast.

She stroked his hair, playing for time, seeking the right way to tell him the truth without hurting either his memory of Sally or his current situation with his father.

"Your mommy and daddy lived far away from each other," was all she could manage for now. It was lame, and she knew someday Wyatt would have to come up with a more satisfying answer, which would create its own problems. "And your mommy couldn't travel much because she was working and didn't have a good car. Then she got sick." She figured the more information and 'excuses' she piled on the fewer questions he might ask. Her own thoughts about Sally had taken a huge U-turn after finding out how Dean was conceived. No wonder her friend had been so elusive about Dean's father.

Dean nodded and gave her a quick smile. "I'm happy we're here all together."

This created another twinge of guilt that Adele pushed down.

But even as she did, her thoughts drifted to the kiss she and Wyatt had shared. The teasing of possibilities.

She swallowed, pushing them down. She couldn't allow herself to indulge in that. Hadn't her life taught her the danger of allowing connections to grow?

She kissed Dean's forehead again, then stood. Could she leave him here?

There's no place for you here. You have your own plans you have to follow through on.

Besides, Leah was counting on her to start this new bakery, and there was no way she was letting her down. She knew too well what it felt like to be abandoned. She certainly wasn't doing that to anyone else.

She closed the door to Dean's room, forcing down her emotions, reminding herself to be practical. Before she went downstairs, she stopped in at the girls' room. They were each in their own bed, fast asleep. Maria had kicked her blankets off, so

Adele pulled them up and tucked them under her chin. Maria's eyes drifted open and she smiled up at Adele. "I love you." Her sleep-slurred words created an ache that, combined with Adele's own mixed emotions, thickened her throat.

"Go to sleep, sweetheart," she whispered, giving in to an impulse and pressing a gentle kiss to her forehead.

Then, shaking off the motherly feelings that curled through her stomach, she made her way downstairs.

Wyatt still sat on the couch, but he had a photo album on his lap.

She sat down in a chair across from him, tucking her legs under her.

"I'm looking at baby pictures of me and my family," Wyatt said, his voice quiet, contemplative. I don't know if I'm just imagining it, or if it's real, but I've got to admit, Dean looks like I did when I was little." He held up the photo book. "Like this."

Adele hesitated, then walked around the coffee table between them and sat down beside him, looking at the grouping of pictures of several young boys. They wore blue jeans and torn T-shirts. One of them held a frog in his hand, the other two were looking closely at it. "Is this you?" she asked, pointing to the middle boy.

"Yep. For some reason, I loved frogs. My brothers, not so much."

"Which one is which?"

"The one on my left is Reuben, the other is Finn. My sister, Carly, was probably running away, screaming. She was such a girl."

"Is that an observation or an insult?" Adele asked, unable to stifle her smile at his comment.

"Not an insult, though when Finn called her that, it could be," Wyatt said with a shrug, glancing over the other pictures on the page. "But we teased the living daylights out of the poor kid. That's her there." He pointed to a picture of a young girl wearing an oversized cowboy hat, a tumble of wild blonde curls falling around her shoulders. She had her hands on her hips and a wry smile on her face.

"She looks like she's ready to take on the world."

"She was, and she did. She has an intense sense of injustice. There was a young boy who used to get teased on the school bus. One time a bunch of older boys were throwing stuff at him. I remember her jumping off her seat and confronting those boys—she was maybe half their size. She was only eight. Shamed me and my brothers into joining her even though the boys were in high school. They backed down though they cornered me and Reuben after school and roughed us up. But they didn't bother that boy after that. Carly never backed down from a fight or a cause she saw as unjust. Smart as a whip."

"Is she around yet?"

Wyatt shook his head. "Not anymore. She left after...well, she's gone for now. I'm hoping she comes back soon. She said she might."

"And you and Reuben?"

"We stuck around." Wyatt was quiet, still studying the pictures.

She looked to the next page, smiling at what she saw.

"I'm guessing that's the whole bunch?" she asked, looking at the large picture that dominated the page.

It was a casual photo. Wyatt and his siblings and, she guessed, his parents. They stood in the middle of a horse pasture, horses gathered around them. The kids were lined up in front of their parents, and Mom and Dad had a hand on each child's shoulder.

"What a beautiful family," Adele said. "When was that taken?"

Wyatt grew serious, staring at the picture. "About half a year before my mother died."

Adele looked more closely at the family. "You couldn't have been over thirteen, I'm guessing."

"I was twelve, Reuben was eleven."

"So young. What happened?"

Wyatt ran his finger over the picture, tracing his mother's features. "My mom got breast cancer. She died eight months later. She wasn't one to run to the doctor, so by the time they discovered the cancer, it had spread too far for them to do anything."

"I'm so sorry to hear that. That must've been difficult for you and your family."

Wyatt nodded. "Dad was devastated. He and Mom were always so close. They did everything together. Even chores on the ranch. She'd help him needle cows, mother orphaned calves, make hay, and still take care of us four kids. She was one tough woman."

Adele's heart contracted at the love and affection in Wyatt's voice. "She sounds amazing."

"She was. We missed her a lot. We all pitched in to keep things going as much as possible, but it was hard for all of us."

"And your father? When did he die?"

"He passed away after Maya and Maria were born. The doctors said it was an advanced form of pneumonia, but Carly always said that he died of a broken heart. He wasn't even that old."

"And what about Reuben? Does he still live around here?"

"Reuben got married half a year before I did. We ranched together until, well, until his wife died of pneumonia. Complications from a car accident that debilitated her." Wyatt shook his head, releasing a harsh laugh. "So many losses."

Adele heard the bitterness in his voice and commiserated with him. She knew loss as well, although it wasn't the same kind as Wyatt's. But it was still loss.

"So that's Reuben," she said pointing to the tall skinny kids standing beside Wyatt. "I'm guessing this is Finn?"

"Yeah. He's the least complicated of all of us. He just enjoys traveling and working to pay for the traveling. I keep telling him he's got to settle down someday. He had a serious girlfriend once, but she didn't like his wandering ways and he wasn't ready to commit. He always says when he finds the right person and reason, he will."

"And what about Carly?"

Wyatt shot her a puzzled smile. "You sure seem interested in my family."

Adele shrugged. "I was an only child. Extended families intrigue me."

"Even in the foster home you were at?"

"Yeah. Bonnie and Earl were an older couple. Never had kids."

"As for my sister, well, Carly's had her own sorrows. She was engaged to a great guy. We all liked him. But he got caught up in drugs. Got busted and ended up in jail for a few years. Carly was devastated. So were we. She broke up with him. I don't know if she's ever gotten over Derek. That's why she left. Said she needed a break from Millar's Crossing and the heaviness here."

"Sounds like your family has had its struggles," she said, feeling a rush of sympathy for him. He sounded sad when he spoke of his sister.

Wyatt sat back, the photo album still open on his lap, but his eyes looking off into space. "Yeah. I used to wonder if God had it in for us. We had a lot of rough patches. But I've been able to see His hand in our lives. How He's taken care of us. Reuben is coming back to the ranch in a couple of months, and once that happens, who knows? Together we might be able to talk Finn into returning. Maybe even Carly." He smiled at the thought and she, once again, envied him his siblings and the closeness they seemed to share. Then he turned to her. "I've given you my family history, what about you? You said you know your way around the ranch, that you learned that from your foster parents. I'm sensing there's a story there too."

Adele sat back, her shoulder brushing his. She knew she should move away, but she wasn't ready to break the connection that had grown between them. It felt good to be sitting close to him.

Especially as she returned to her own past.

"How did you end up in a foster home? Do you want to talk about it?" he pressed, but his voice was gentle. His sensitivity warmed the empty and lonely part of her soul that missed having someone care about her.

"I don't mind, but it's hard," she admitted, folding her arms over her chest, as if to protect herself.

"You mentioned a father. What about your mother?"

"My mother died shortly after I was born, and I think my father never got over that. The first couple years of my life I spent in a foster home, or so I've been told. I don't remember anything about that. My dad came back for me when I was about two and a half and brought me home again."

"Where was home?"

"In the Fairview area. Up north."

"Where your foster parents lived," Wyatt said.

Adele nodded, her thoughts sifting back.

"Did your father own a ranch?" he asked, his voice quiet. Encouraging.

"A farm," she corrected with a wry look. "Not big, but enough to support us. I think he tried at first to keep things going after my mother died. But I'm sure he was dealing with some type of depression. I can say that now, as an adult looking back. But as a child, it was incredibly difficult to deal with."

Adele looked down, trying to find the right words to explain her life without falling into self-pity. "I think my dad was kinda like your dad. He never got over losing my mom. But unfortunately, he chose a different way to handle it." She paused, trying to find the right tone to explain. The right words. Then decided to go with straightforward and true. "He drank a lot."

"How old were you when that started?"

"He always drank some, but it got worse when I was about ten. That's when he started staying away longer. Spending more money."

"So young," he said, his voice quiet.

"I had to grow up quick. But I had a neighbor who watched out for me even though my father said she was just being snoopy. She was in a wheelchair or, she said, she would have taken me herself. She called Social Services. I was fortunate. I got put into the Stefanski home, the one I was in before. I was there for three months that time." She stopped, not sure what else he wanted to hear. She was suddenly aware that she was telling him more than she had told her few closest friends.

"That time. I'm sensing there were more?"

"Many more. Each time I would go back, my father would promise things would get better and they didn't. When he lost his part-time job at the sawmill, things became terrible." She was embarrassed to hear the small hitch in her voice and she hoped Wyatt missed it. She didn't enjoy feeling sorry for herself. Thanks to Bonnie and Earl she had learned to be grateful in all the circumstances of her life.

"Did your father ever hurt you?"

She let her thoughts sift back to the few times he would come back to the house blind drunk. How he would be sobbing, crying. Then he would see Adele and his eyes would narrow. As if she caused all his troubles.

"He tried a few times. But he was so drunk he could hardly stand straight. It didn't take much to avoid him."

Again, she aimed for the jokey tone that often deflected further questions. But to her surprise, she felt Wyatt's arm slip around her shoulders. Give her a gentle hug. "That must have been terrifying."

She let her thoughts settle on the old memories, surprised she had let herself wander this far back. Usually she stopped herself. She couldn't afford to drop too deep into the past. Too often when the dark thoughts came, she was on her own.

But somehow, sitting close to Wyatt, feeling his warmth beside her, the weight of his strong arm around her, created a sense of safety even as the wind whistled around the exterior of the house. She was safe here. Secluded.

"It was. I remember phoning my foster parents the second time. They were at the house in minutes. They took me to their place, and I never had to go back to my father's again." Her throat thickened. "They loved me so much. They were so good to me. I didn't deserve what they gave me."

"Why not? Why would you say that?" As he asked the question, she felt the fingers of his other hand brush the hair away from her face, then his hand cupped her chin, turning her face to his.

She knew they were dancing dangerously close to a moment they would have a hard time coming back from.

The last time he kissed her, she knew it couldn't happen again.

She had to stop this.

And yet, with her soul and heart bruised by the old memories and the old guilt rising, the questions that could haunt her needed an out, and he was right here.

"I didn't love them as much as I should have," was all she could say, his eyes only a foot from hers. "I missed my dad and...and he didn't deserve to be missed. I loved them but I always felt that they didn't know how much I did. I used to cry when I was there and I know they felt bad when I did. They gave me so much—" Her voice broke. She tried to stop herself, knowing it was senseless to go back, to try to reconstruct and rebuild what was over and done.

"Of course you would miss your father," he said, his thumb

stroking her chin. "You knew him when, I'm sure, he was a better man. And you probably kept hoping that man would come back. And that man would take you home."

His words gave voice to thoughts she could never articulate herself. And as she held his gaze, she felt a rush of gratitude. His eyes were like a deep well of consolation she didn't even know she had desired for so long.

"I think that's exactly it," she said, blinking back a sudden and unwelcome rush of tears. She tried to swallow them down, but when Wyatt's thumb gently wiped at her cheek, she knew she had failed.

"I'm so sorry you had to deal with that," he said.

She didn't know what to say in return. But despite the warnings clanging through her mind, her hand came up to his shoulder and she moved closer to him, wanting to extend the connection, to build on it. To get even closer.

Then she was pulled closer, his mouth fitted over hers, his arms pressing her against his strong and solid warmth. She responded, her heart soaring in her chest, beating in time to his. His mouth was warm, gentle, and as their lips moved over each other, a deeper yearning rose within her. She wrapped her arms around him, unable to hold him close enough, to kiss him hard enough.

They slowly pulled away, but Wyatt pressed his forehead to hers, still holding her close. His breathing was shallow, quick, and she could tell he was as moved by their kiss as she had been.

He swallowed and reluctantly she drew back, framing his face with her hand to maintain their connection.

For a long moment their eyes were lost in each others', as if seeking more.

Then she pulled back even more, giving herself some distance, but staying close to him.

Neither spoke for a long moment, as if words would only break what had just happened.

He caught her hand in his, stroking it, looking down. He found the bumpy scar on the side of her thumb and traced it gently. "Where did this come from?" he asked, concern tingeing his voice.

"I got it when I was putting up barb-wire fence with Earl. I wanted to help and he was willing to let me. But my gloves slipped off as I was lifting up a roll." She smiled at the memory. "He felt terrible. I thought he would cry. Despite the pain it caused, it made me feel good that I mattered. That was new for me."

Wyatt frowned, and she regretted saying that. She didn't want to seem as she was feeling sorry for herself.

"You've had a difficult childhood." He said the words simply, stating a fact.

"I've had some great times too," she returned, trying to pull herself out of the self-pity that she struggled daily not to fall into. "My foster parents loved me and gave me everything my father couldn't or wouldn't."

"Is your father still around?"

"No. He died in a car accident when I was sixteen. Thankfully, it was a single vehicle accident, because he was drunk."

"And how long were you with your foster parents?"

"Until I was eighteen." She stopped, her emotions still too tender. Too close to the surface.

"Why did you leave then?"

She wished he hadn't asked but appreciated his concern. And because of that, and with him sitting right beside her, creating a sense of peace and safety, she allowed herself to carry on. "Because that's when my foster father died. Bonnie was so distraught. Everything fell apart then. She sold the farm and moved in with her sister. Who didn't want me around."

"So you were on your own?"

"I had finished high school early, so I was okay. I know Bonnie felt horrible and wished she could have helped me out, but she was stuck too. And grieving. I was thankful for the home she and Earl gave me. I probably would have moved out in a few months anyway. I never had any intention of staying in Fairview." She gave him a quick smile. "Like every other kid in my graduating class, my motto was 'Get the heck out of Dodge.'"

"Sounds like my family," Wyatt said, giving her a gentle smile as he leaned back on the couch, creating a small distance between them. "I never wanted to leave the ranch though. I was happy to stay and work with my dad."

She gave him a careful smile. "You say you feel bad for me, but you've had more than your share of sorrows too."

"I'll admit that," he said. "But I had a strong family bond and a good community to support me. Sounds like you didn't."

She couldn't believe how easily he shifted from his own situation to hers.

"I had good friends the past three years."

"Like Sally."

Just bringing her name into the conversation was like a dose of reality.

Sally's son sleeping upstairs with Wyatt's daughters. Wyatt's family and his responsibilities.

"I feel like I have to apologize for her behavior all those years ago-"

"You had nothing to do with that," he told her.

"I know. But it was wrong of her."

"Who knows what she was dealing with? And like the old saying, it takes two."

Adele nodded, wondering why Sally had never told her the truth. Then she realized it wouldn't have mattered. Dean was still here.

Adele eased away from him and caught Wyatt's frown. She wanted to act casual but realized she may as well be honest and straightforward. "I'm thinking about the kids."

Wyatt grew serious then, seeming to be on the same wavelength as her. "You're thinking we have to be careful."

"I am."

He eased out a sigh, resting his head against the back of the couch, but keeping his eyes on her. "I realize that too, but I'm not going to lie. I believe something is happening between us. Something special."

That he felt it too made her heart want to sing.

"Do you think it might just be loneliness?" She had to ask. Had to put everything out on the table. There was too much at risk. Her heart. Her future. His children.

He didn't answer right away, and she wondered if he thought she was trying to retreat from this.

"I don't think so. Unless that's the case for you."

She held his gaze, allowing the emotions she felt around him to rise again, and then shook her head. "I don't think so, either."

"Well, then we'll just have to see how things progress."

He sounded so practical, she had to smile.

Then he touched her face, his fingers lingering. She wondered if he would kiss her again. Wished he would. But then his hand shifted to hers and he stood, pulling her up with him.

"I don't know about you, but I'm tired. So I'm saying good night."

Then he did kiss her again. A gentle brush of his lips over her forehead. It was enough, and yet not enough.

But she realized that they needed to move slowly. Carefully.

So she brushed her hand over his cheek and then turned away from him before she changed her mind.

The scent of supper cooking greeted Wyatt as he came into the house Monday evening. It made his mouth water and his heart warm.

The nanny he had hired only worked until four, so he was usually on his own with the girls for supper.

Theresa's idea of cooking was heating hot dogs or chicken strips. If he wanted anything different, he had to cook it himself.

Tonight his house smelled like the home his mother kept.

He sat down, tugged his heavy winter boots off, and then pulled off his coveralls. Snow still crusted the bottoms of the coveralls and his boots. Inevitable, considering how much had come down the past few days. He had tried to shovel the sidewalk a couple of times, but it was a herculean effort to move all that snow.

Adele wouldn't be leaving any time soon.

The thought created a mixture of emotions. Relief on the one hand. Concern on the other. After last night he knew they had stepped over a line that would be hard to come back from.

He had his daughters to think about, he reminded himself as he set his boots on the boot rack. And now, Dean.

Wyatt blew out his breath, still adjusting to the reality of Dean being his son. *That will take some doing*, he said to himself.

"Daddy, you're here," Maya announced, leaning into the porch. "We are having supper soon."

"Well, then it's good I came in when I did," he said, picking her up and giving her a tight hug.

"Oooh, you're all cold," she said, bracketing his cheeks with her hands. "And your hair is wet."

"From the snow," he said, setting her down away from the melting snow on the porch floor. "It's still snowing out there."

"We can go sliding," she announced, grabbing his hand and leading him into the house.

"No, honey. It's too windy and snowy out there yet." Wyatt's eyes slipped to Adele, who stood by the counter, chopping up vegetables for salad. She looked up at him in that same moment, and once again he had this feeling of time stopping.

A sense that everything and everyone around them fell away, and it was just the two of them.

Then he blinked, and she looked away and the feeling left.

But the memory stayed.

"I imagine the driveway is still blown in," Adele said, her voice gruff, her head now bent to her task.

"Yes. It would take me at least two days to clear it out if it wasn't storming, and with the snow still coming down, it's not worth doing."

"I heard a report on the radio that the county roads are still impassable."

"I imagine the school busses aren't running either."

"No. I just heard a notice coming in on the radio."

Wyatt had to smile. He remembered his parents having the same kind of conversation in this very kitchen. Ordinary talk about life.

"Look at my picture," Maria said, holding up a piece of paper that she'd been coloring. Bright pink and purple streaks filled the image he suspected Adele had printed off for her.

"That's great," he said, crouching down beside her. "You did such a good job."

"She didn't stay in the lines," Maya said, frowning at her sister's attempt.

"She picked pretty colors," Dean put in, looking up from the cowboy picture he was working on.

Wyatt's heart warmed to the little boy's compliment, counteracting Maya's criticism.

"She certainly did." He smiled at Dean, who looked shyly up at him. Probably still not sure where to put this man in his life.

That makes two of us, Wyatt thought. He gave in to an impulse, however, and touched Dean's shoulder, letting his fingers rest there, creating a small connection.

His reward was a beaming smile.

He's an easy kid to love, he thought.

"Sorry to tell you kids this, but we need to clear the table for dinner," Adele announced, coming to join the group.

"We're having sgetti," Maria said as she obediently gathered up the crayons.

"That's great. I love sgetti almost as much as I love spaghetti," Wyatt said, unable to resist another sidelong glance at Adele. She was laughing, and the sight warmed his heart.

"I want to finish my picture," Maya announced, bent over her paper, her tongue peeking out from between her lips.

"Adele said we have to clean up." Dean dropped his crayons in the tin on the table.

"Don't want to," Maya said.

"We have to listen to Adele," Dean put in.

"I don't. She's not my mom." Maya's tone was more matter of fact than rebellious. "And you're not my mom."

"Doesn't matter, Maya. Adele asked you to do something and you need to do it," Wyatt said.

Maya kept her head down, and Wyatt could see her lips were now pressed tightly together. A sure sign that a rebellion was brewing.

"Sweetie, what are you going to do?" he asked.

"Keep coloring."

And here it was. That hard disobedience that rose up from time to time. The pushback Wyatt wasn't always sure how to deal with.

He laid his hand on her shoulder, pressing gently. "Maya, you need to listen and obey."

But she was ignoring him, her crayon moving furiously across the paper.

Oh brother, now what? He looked over at Adele, who seemed as uncertain as he was on how to proceed, and gave her a faint shrug.

"Okay, Maya," Adele said, taking her cue from him. "You can keep coloring, or you can have dinner. Up to you."

No answer.

The other two children were watching them, as if wondering what would happen next.

Adele helped Dean and Maria put their papers away, leaving the tin of crayons on the table.

"I think we'll have our supper in the family room," Adele said, smiling at the other two. She glanced over at Wyatt. "If that's okay with you?"

He realized what she was doing. Letting Maya have her way and yet not let her control the situation. His admiration for her grew. Usually he was too tired to deal with Maya's stubbornness. Thankfully, her rebellious times were few, but she was only three. He knew more would be coming.

"I think that's a great idea. Maybe we can watch some television."

At that, Maya looked up, her eyes narrowed as if unsure of how things were progressing.

Adele didn't even look at her as she walked over to the stove, taking the plates she had laid out and serving up the spaghetti and meatballs.

"Careful now," she warned Dean and Maria as they took their plates to the family room.

The two kids looked smug as they walked past Maya, who wasn't coloring anymore, watching them with puzzlement.

Not how this was supposed to turn out, is it, Wyatt thought, grinning at her confusion.

When Wyatt got his plate and headed toward the family room, Maya jumped off her chair. "You can't eat there. You eat here."

He shrugged, glancing back at Adele, who already had her plate of food served up. "No. You have your crayons on the table," Wyatt said. "There's no room. And you want to keep coloring, so you go ahead."

Maya blinked, watching as they walked past her.

"No. No. I want to eat," she said.

"I thought you wanted to color?" Adele asked.

"I do. But I'm hungry now."

"You can have some food after you clean up your coloring," Adele returned, her voice quiet. Gentle and even.

Maya's eyes narrowed as she glanced from Adele to the table behind her. She wavered, and Wyatt wondered to himself how this would end.

Then Maya spun around and, to his surprise, made quick work of cleaning up, even bringing the crayon tin and her papers to the end of the counter.

"I eat now," she announced.

"Can you please say that a bit nicer?" Adele prodded.

Wyatt thought she might be pushing her luck, but to his surprise, Maya nodded. "Please, can I eat now?"

"Of course. I'll just take my plate to the family room, and then I'll get you your supper."

Wyatt was full of admiration for how Adele handled the situation. He had wondered how this would all play out, but Adele seemed to know what she was doing. She had a knack for dealing with kids.

He followed Adele, forcing himself not to look back at Maya to catch her reaction. Adele wasn't dancing to her tune, and he knew Maya was confused.

Adele was as good as her word, and soon they were all sitting around the television, eating their supper. Dean, Maya, and Maria sat on the floor, their plates on the coffee table, watching the television as they ate.

"I hope this is okay," Adele whispered to Wyatt.

"Too late to ask me now, isn't it?" he teased.

"Well, I'm sorry. I should have checked with you." She lifted her hand in a gesture of apology.

He caught her hand and gave it a gentle squeeze. "It's fine. I'm just amazed at how you handled her, that's all. I have to confess, I was lost." He kept his voice low, hoping the kids were too engrossed in their television show to pay them any mind. "How did you know what to do?"

"Something I learned from Earl when he was training horses."

Wyatt grinned, curious. "And what was that?"

"Make it easy for them to do what you want them to do and hard for them to do what you don't want them to do."

This made him chuckle. "Sounds like I should have spent more time training horses so I could apply that to raising kids."

"I'm sure there are some differences," Adele said. "But sometimes Dean can get as goofy as some of Earl's horses."

Wyatt looked over at the kids who were eating, their eyes glued to the television. "You sure are good with kids."

Adele shrugged, but from her smile, Wyatt could see she didn't take offense to his comment.

"I like kids. And I know you do too."

"I should. I have two...three of them now." He caught himself just in time, his eyes on Dean, who was busy watching television.

Adele was quiet, as if sensing where his thoughts were going.

They said nothing until their plates were empty, and then without a word, Adele stood and cleared up. Wyatt was about to follow her when she shook her head. "Just sit with the kids," she said.

He guessed what she was trying to do. Allow him as much time as possible to be with Dean and his daughters on his own.

He sat, watching them. They still sat on the floor, still watched the silly television show.

The storm outside howled, but despite the trouble it caused, it also created a cozy feeling.

He was in his home, with his family.

And a beautiful woman had made them a delicious supper. The house felt like a home, and that was no small thing to him.

He got up and grabbed some books from the bookshelf, standing in front of the television to get the kids' attention. "Five more minutes, and then I'm turning it off and I'll read you some stories," he said.

Maya ignored him, craning her neck to look past him. Maria also ignored him, but to his surprise Dean stood, looking at him. "Can we read now?" he asked.

"Not now," Maria announced. "Five minutes."

Wyatt shook his head at his daughters' obsession with television. Clearly Dean didn't share it, something that created a flash of admiration for the little guy.

"I can read a book to you now if you want," Wyatt said.

Dean gave him a careful smile and scooted over to the couch. Wyatt sat down beside him. Dean kept some distance between them, looking uncertain. The small gesture created a tiny ache in Wyatt's heart. Poor kid. Still dealing with so much, now dropped into an unfamiliar household with an unfamiliar man he had hoped would be his father.

"This first book is about a construction site getting ready to go to sleep." Denise, Reuben's wife, had given it to him. She said it was probably more of a boy's book, but the girls loved the rhythms of the language, and he often read it to them at bedtime. It was a huge hit, and Wyatt loved reading the series as well. The other book was about a train, and the third was about a small skid steer.

He opened the book and angled it so Dean could see the pictures and began reading. He lowered his voice, and Dean leaned in to hear better, his eyes on the pages of the book. As he read, he glanced down at Dean from time to time, and slowly the boy moved in a little closer. He was halfway through the book when Dean was snuggled right up against him. Wyatt turned the page slowly, trying to get his wits about him. Dean's easy trust, his connection with him, gave him a tiny hitch in his heart. He swallowed down an unexpected emotion, took a breath, and carried on.

When he was finished, Dean looked up at him with a smile. "Thanks. I like that book a lot. Can you read it again?"

"Of course."

He lifted his arm, a small invitation, and Dean slipped his own hand through it. Just for a few seconds, it was just him and this boy. His son.

This will work, he thought. This could work. He sent up a prayer of thanks and turned the book to the beginning again.

"Read to us, read to us," Maya called out, noticing what was going on. "No fair."

"You wanted to watch television," Wyatt said.

"No television. You read." Maya grabbed the remote and clicked the button to shut it off.

His girls knew too much about how to work the television. Not the best commentary on his parenting.

"Okay, but I'm reading the books I picked out," Wyatt warned.

Maria nabbed her place on the other side of Wyatt and, to his surprise, Maya seemed content to sit beside Dean.

He took a moment to glance at the grouping of kids, surprised again at how easily things seemed to be shifting. Thankful for this small moment.

And then he heard Adele busy in the kitchen and he wondered if he dared allow her into his life as well. He had been so wrong about Theresa. Did he dare trust his judgment? Did he dare open his heart again?

CHAPTER TEN

$\mathcal{A}$ dele hovered in the doorway of the family room, watching Wyatt read to the kids.

If anyone was a natural parent, it was him.

He raised and lowered his voice as he read, looking to the kids once in a while, pausing from time to time to let the kids finish the sentences. The girls seemed to know the story well. They called out the right words and earned a smile from Wyatt in return.

He even got Dean to read some words, running his finger under them and encouraging him to look at the pictures.

The sight both warmed her heart and created a sense of loss. Dean was being amalgamated into this family. It was what she wanted and what he needed.

Then why did she feel this quiver of jealousy?

And beneath that, a remembrance of happier times with her foster mother who read to her even though Adele could read the books herself.

She loved curling up beside Bonnie and having her read. She

would lay her head on Bonnie's shoulder and let the words captivate and transport her.

And now, Dean was on the receiving end of all this. So much more than Adele could even think of giving him.

She swallowed at the thought of leaving him behind.

Do you have to?

The question slipped so easily into her mind; it was as if it had been there for days. Hovering, waiting for the right time.

She shook her head to dislodge it. She couldn't stay. She had her plans. Her own future to think of.

But you and Wyatt...

She watched him, allowing herself a few moments of *what if.* Thinking of the kisses they shared.

That's not enough to build on. That's just loneliness.

But even as her practical mind chastised her and brought reality into the moment, her heart knew more than that was going on. She had dated before. Had been attracted to other men.

But no man had ever created the intense feelings Wyatt did. Made her feel a sense of rightness.

No man had ever made her doubt her plans and her own future.

You can't allow anyone to derail you again. How many times have your plans had to change because of your father? How many dreams have you had to let die?

She closed her eyes, her head fighting with her heart. Dream versus reality. She and Sally had spent hours, days, weeks, months, planning this. Now she was carrying this on with Leah. This was her shot at an independent life. A way of taking care of herself that didn't involve adjusting to an unreasonable boss's demands. A man's whims and wishes. If she didn't follow through—

"Why don't you come join us?"

Wyatt's gentle voice interrupted her thoughts, and she pulled herself back to the present.

She hesitated, but then Dean looked over at her, smiling, and combined with Wyatt's invitation, she gave in. Wyatt, she had to be careful around, but Dean had her wrapped around his finger.

"I'm finishing this book and then I think it's bedtime, right?" Wyatt asked her.

She glanced at her watch and nodded. "Pretty soon."

"Two more books," Maria pressed. "Adele, you read one too."

"No. Let your dad read," Adele said, lowering herself into the love seat across from the couch they all sat on. "He does such a good job."

"Come sit here," Maya insisted, patting the couch between her and Dean.

"I've got one you can read if you want," Wyatt put in, smiling his own encouragement.

Adele was about to wave off his suggestion when Dean added his own request. "Please, Adele?"

Again, she was like putty with the little guy, so with a shrug, she got up and settled between Dean and Maya. Maria clambered onto Wyatt's lap as Adele took the book from him.

This one was about a little mouse who just wanted to be left alone to read his favorite books. Adele had never seen it before and had to smile at the beautiful illustrations.

The entire time she was reading she was conscious of Wyatt, sitting beside Dean. Out of the corner of her eye, she saw him slip his arm around Dean, letting his hand rest on her shoulder. Awareness shivered through her. But beneath all that, there was a feeling of comfort and belonging. This felt so right. So true.

The storm that had stranded them raged on, but here, in this place, in this moment, peace and contentment reigned.

She finished the last book she intended to read, and the kids clamored for another one, but it was late.

"Sorry, guys, now it's really time for bed," Wyatt said, as if he could read her thoughts.

All three of them looked to Adele, but she shrugged. "Sorry. Dad says it's bedtime."

As soon as she spoke, she realized that she sounded like any wife and mother talking to her children. It was too late to take it back now. Wyatt said nothing as he gathered up the books.

"I'll tuck them in," he said to Adele, giving her a gentle smile.

She nodded, the peace she had felt before seeping back into the moment.

And as he went up the stairs with the children, she felt a tiny yearning to follow him.

"And here's one for you," Adele said, dropping the paper hat she'd just made on Dean's head.

He turned his head left and right as if trying it on for size. "I like it. I feel like a pirate."

"You look exactly like a pirate," she said, gathering up the rest of the newspapers.

It was late Tuesday and Adele had spent most of the afternoon keeping the kids occupied. She didn't want them watching television all day, but it was convenient while she cleaned up and got food ready for supper.

Wyatt had been outside most of the day working on waterers, clearing snow off the yard for the cows so he could feed them. He also had some work to do on the tractor. Apparently one of the bale forks had broken off in the cold weather so he had to weld it back on. She had seen him through the blinding snow at one time trying to push what he could off the driveway, but it drifted in right behind him again.

At any rate it kept him busy most of the day. He came in at lunchtime, snatched a quick bite to eat, and then left again. He needed to get as much done as he could before dark. He had apologized to her, asking if she was okay with him being gone. While she was thankful for the distance his busyness created, she found she missed him. But she couldn't expect him to hang around the house all day when he had work to do.

Just as he left, though, he had given her a careful smile. A small connection. An enlarging of what had happened between them.

"And this is your hat," she said to Maya, who had been dancing about while waiting for her turn. She opened it up and put it on her head.

"This is not a princess hat," she said with a frown, pulling the hat off.

"It will be once you color some stars on it," Adele said.

Maya turned the hat around in her hand then with a heavy sigh set it on the table and pulled out a marker. "I will make it pretty."

Maria was happy to have her newspaper hat look the same as Dean's. The two of them were pretending to be fighting with the swords Adele had made out of rolled up newspaper.

The casserole she had worked on was in the oven. She knew Wyatt would be coming in for supper at about six o'clock. Despite the storm that had been the routine of the past few days.

With a sigh she glanced out the window. Though it had only been two days, she felt incredibly house-bound. The kids had been great, though they had begged to play outside. Adele had talked them out of it with promises to make cookies that were now cooling on the counter, ready for dessert with supper.

"Why don't you guys go downstairs with your swords," Adele suggested.

The basement was unfinished and wide open, giving the kids lots of room to play.

"Yay, we can make a boat out of the box," Dean called out.

The little girls were right behind him, and Adele had a moment of peace.

She gathered up the newspapers. A series of pictures caught her attention and made her smile. A little boy sliding down the slide in the park, togue askew on his head. In the second one he hit the ground, sending up a cloud of snow.

The caption said the boy was Todd Corbett.

The name meant nothing to her, but it was so cute she had to smile.

She wondered how old he was. If he would be in the same grade as Dean when he started school.

An unexpected sorrow pierced her heart. Dean would live here. Go to school here.

Wyatt would be taking care of him.

She shook off the thoughts, folding the papers, skimming the news as she did.

Then she frowned when she saw another article. It was about a bakery in town that had been closed for the past half year. A series of photos depicting the bakery through the years. Three generations of Chernowyks had run the bakery. Victor, the brother of the last owner, expressed regret that no one was willing to take it over.

A note on the bottom mentioned the listing was in the advertisement and sales section.

Adele flipped through the papers, wondering if she had used that page for the kids.

But she found the correct page and her eyes skimmed the listings.

Her heart gave a little skip when she saw it.

Bakery for sale.

It stated that the equipment came with the building but could be sold if needed. The listing was long, laying out all the equipment. Adele ran her finger down it, surprised at the wealth of supplies that would come with. The ovens were older than the one on the auction site she and Leah were looking at, but it came with more supplies.

She couldn't stop the faint lift of excitement when she saw everything listed. A baker's dream.

However, there was no price. Interested parties were to contact the real estate agent.

Adele shot a quick glance at the clock. She had time before the office closed. An hour before Wyatt returned.

The kids were busy downstairs.

Before she could talk herself out of it, she snatched her phone and dialed. The phone rang and rang and rang.

Hang up. You have a plan with Leah. You can't back out of it.

She let it ring one more time then hung up, shaking off her second thoughts.

But before she threw the papers away, she ripped out the ad, folded it up, and put it in her pocket.

Wyatt hunkered down against the storm, adding more split wood to the pile he'd been building up for the past hour.

With the storm blowing as steadily as it had, the odds of the power going off grew. And he didn't want to split wood in the dark.

Now he was done. A decent pile of wood nestled on the deck, in the lee of the porch overhang.

He moved the snow machine closer to the shelter of the house and turned it off. Snow would probably bury it tomorrow, but this way it would be handy if he needed to get anywhere on the yard. He shivered, glancing back at the snow still slanting sideways across the yard. Thankfully, the snow fences he had put up in the cattle yards were working, and he got through the drifts to put out more straw for the cows. But he sure hoped this weather would ease soon.

Filling his arms with wood, he stamped the snow off his boots as best he could, then stepped inside, dropping the kindling and the wood into the cradle in the porch. He had been busy all day, struggling between feeling guilty that Adele was taking care of his kids and the need to get the tractor up and running again.

But even as he was working, his hands busy, his mind kept shifting to Adele.

He dropped the last piece of firewood onto the pile, took off his coat and coveralls, then walked into the house, his eyes lighting on Adele. She sat at the table, staring off into space, frowning.

She looked worried, and he wondered what she was thinking.

He felt as if they had been walking carefully through the past few days. Trying to balance their situation with their changing feelings.

"Oh, hey. You're early," she said, looking up at him, her smile settling into his heart.

"Yeah. I was done, so I thought I would come to the house."

"Of course. I didn't mean..." She paused, her hands fluttering as she stood. "I was just...you said you'd be here at six."

"Sorry."

"No. No." She sounded flustered. "You've been working all day. Of course you would want to come in the house." She stopped there, shaking her head. "Now I'm sorry. I sound like a complete dunce. Just caught me unawares. We can eat right away."

Her scattered tone gave him pause, but he caught himself. *Don't overthink this. She was just off in her own world for a while.*

"Where are the kids?" he asked.

"Downstairs. Playing pirate."

"I imagine they're going a bit stir crazy."

"Not too bad," she said, pulling plates out of the cupboard.

"We've been keeping ourselves occupied, though I sure hope this storm quits soon."

Right. She had to leave on Friday for the auction sale.

"Supper is ready. You can get the kids."

Maya and Maria were chasing Dean around the empty basement, brandishing rolled-up newspapers, yelling like little banshees.

So very ladylike, he thought, chuckling at the sight.

"Hey. Don't be so hard on the poor guy," he said as Maya ran past him.

"He's the bad pirate," she called out.

Dean was laughing though. Again Wyatt marveled at how good the little boy was with his daughters. How he tolerated them.

And he wondered what they would be like in a few years.

The thought grabbed him, bringing the reality of Dean's presence harder home. The boy would grow up here. Would go to school here.

And how would he explain that to the family?

He hadn't even told his brothers and sister yet.

It was as if, since Adele had come, his world had not only been turned upside down, it had narrowed. Grown small.

Sooner or later he would have to step outside this bubble.

And where would Adele be then?

But even as the questions hovered, he knew her plans were becoming more important to him.

"Time for supper," he told the kids, shutting down his thoughts. *Too much thinking these days*, he told himself.

The kids didn't protest and followed him upstairs.

Adele had the table set, and the kids all sat down, regaling Wyatt with stories of the books Adele had read, how they had made cookies, and the pirate hats she'd made.

"I hope you saved some paper in case I need to light a fire," Wyatt said, pulling a quiet Adele into the conversation.

She frowned, then bit her lip. "I think I did," she said as she sat down.

"Don't worry," he said. "I was teasing."

She gave an abstracted nod, then held her hand out to Dean and Maria. The signal to say grace.

Wyatt prayed for the food, for people out in the storm, for safety, for the rest of his family. As he finished, he glanced at Dean again and thought of Reuben, Finn, and Carly.

He would have to tell them. Soon.

Tonight, he told himself. Tonight he would let his family know what was happening in his life.

But as he looked over at Adele, who was serving up the kid's plates, he wanted to hold this time close a bit longer.

CHAPTER ELEVEN

"*O*kay, kids. Time for bed."

"One more story," Dean begged, giving Adele his most winning smile.

Seriously, that boy would be trouble when he grew older.

The thought caught Adele by the heart. She wondered how much she would see of that. Would she come back to visit?

Then her eyes flitted to Wyatt sitting on the other side of the couch, the kids between them.

And her thoughts veered into another direction she had been struggling to deal with.

Could she leave?

She thought of the newspaper clipping in her pocket. Thought of the possibilities it represented.

"Please," Dean begged. "You read seven books last night."

"Seven short books," Adele said, glancing at the clock.

After supper, as they had last night, Wyatt had taken the kids to the family room while Adele cleaned up. They had played a few games and when Adele joined them, the kids had a pile of books stacked on the coffee table.

He looked as if he was about to protest again when, suddenly, they were plunged into darkness.

The girls screamed and Adele reached out to them, her eyes slowly adjusting to the dark. "It's okay," she said. "Don't worry. It's just the power going out. It will come back on soon."

As if mocking her, the wind howled outside, easier to hear now that it wasn't drowned out by the earlier sounds of the refrigerator and the furnace blowing.

"What will we do?" Dean's worried voice came out of the darkness.

"Sit tight. I'll get the flashlights," Wyatt said, patting him on the shoulder.

Adele sat down again, pulling the girls onto the couch beside her. In the half gloom she saw Wyatt making his way to the kitchen. A few moments later he was back with two flashlights, sending twin cones of light onto the floor.

"Okay. We're set here." He handed one to Adele. "If you don't need any help with the kids, I'm gonna start a fire."

"Probably a good idea." She had heard him dropping pieces of wood against the house before he came in for supper. Thank goodness he had the foresight to plan for this eventuality. At least the house would be warm.

"We still have to go to bed?" Maria asked.

"It'll be dark," Maya said, her tone matter of fact now that they had light again.

"It's always dark at night," Dean put in. "Always."

"Tell you what, you can all sleep in the same room and I'll stay with you until you're asleep, okay?" Adele said, sounding upbeat. "It'll be like a one-bedroom sleepover."

"That sounds cool," Dean said, taking his cue from her.

"Yay. Sleepover," Maya said, now seeing things differently.

Adele had to chuckle at their excitement.

"Here you go, buddy," she said, handing Dean the flashlight. "You lead the way and we'll follow behind you."

Dean took the flashlight and sent the beam around the room. Then he pointed it to the floor. "Just follow me," he said with an authority that made Adele chuckle.

"Make sure you don't use the water," Wyatt said. "We'll get air in the lines."

"Right. I forgot about that." She had experienced a few power outages when she was living with Earl and Bonnie. She remembered how the taps bucked and snapped when the power would come on again.

She made the children brush their teeth without water, used some wipes to clean their hands and faces, and got them settled in bed.

While she was busy with the kids, she could hear Wyatt downstairs. She heard the crackle of wood, which meant the fire was going.

She tucked the kids in, said their bedtime prayers, and sang a song with them. Then, as she promised, she sat on the floor between the beds to wait for them to go to sleep. At first they giggled and laughed, excited. But soon they settled down, and a few minutes later she could hear the girls breathing deeply.

In the half-light from the flashlight she saw Dean still sitting up in bed.

"You're not tired?" she asked.

"Mr. Wyatt read me a book. It was nice."

The way he addressed Wyatt concerned her, but she wasn't sure she could correct him.

At the same time, however, the DNA test had brought the reality of his paternity home. But how he addressed Wyatt, well, that was not hers to deal with.

"He's a good man," she said instead. "And I know he likes you very much."

Dean nodded, tapping his finger on his chin. A chin she realized, that was much like Wyatt's.

"I like him too," he said. Then he lay down, curling on his side, watching her. "And I like you too."

His words created an odd quiver in her chest. She had so much she wanted to say to him but settled for a simple, "I like you too, sweetheart."

He smiled at that, then snuggled into his blankets. "You don't need to stay with me. I'm not scared."

"I know. You're a very brave boy. But I don't mind staying until you fall asleep."

Though part of her wanted to be downstairs with Wyatt, she knew she was safer up here.

Finally, Dean fell asleep, and she kneeled beside him, stroking his cheek. Then she pressed a kiss to his forehead and stood.

She watched him, struggling with her conflicting emotions.

All her life she had kept her heart safe. Even when she lived with her foster parents, she had been careful with her affections. She had been so used to pain and loss that she always felt she had to hold a piece of her self back. A way to protect herself. But it was tiring, and it made for a lonely existence.

This little boy had wormed his way past her defenses. And she had to leave him behind.

She turned away, a fist pressed to her chest, as if to hold her heart in. Then, as she made her way down the stairs, she saw Wyatt, sitting on the couch. The glow of the fire creating interesting shadows over his face. He had a few candles sitting on the end tables, creating a welcome and intimate flickering light.

And the heart she had spent so long trying to protect, jumped in her chest.

Danger, danger.

Yet she allowed herself to move toward him. But this time she sat on the loveseat opposite. To give herself some space.

"Kids all settled in?" he asked, smiling across the small distance between them.

"All fast asleep. I think they'll be okay."

It would be another long evening, and somehow she had to keep herself occupied. Last night Wyatt had gone into his study after putting the kids in bed and she had retreated to her bedroom with her laptop. Dean had been fast asleep and wasn't bothered by the light of the computer.

Wyatt held up a book. "I'll read, if that's okay with you." Looked like he wouldn't be retreating to his study. Which would make it look awkward if she left. So she nodded, opening her laptop.

Thankfully it was fully charged. She should be good for at least this evening.

She opened a document and settled in, curling her legs up under her.

The plans for the bakery she had been working on flashed on the screen. Usually it gave her a small lift to be working on this. Usually.

But that was before Wyatt. Before the questions he created. Before the advertisement that she still had in the pocket of her blue jeans.

You're a silly girl, her sensible part told herself. She frowned at the screen. *This is reality. You and Leah have plans, and you can't leave her in the lurch. You'll be leaving, and he'll be staying with his three kids.*

But even as she clicked and dragged, rearranging spaces, working on the dream that had kept her saving, working, planning for so long, she was far too aware of the man across the room from her.

And the possibilities he created.

Wyatt watched Adele working on her laptop, wondering what triggered her withdrawal.

Restless, he stood. "I'm making some hot chocolate, you want some?"

She looked up at him and nodded, her smile bridging the gap he had sensed between them. "That would be nice."

He was about to walk to the kitchen when he stopped.

"Right. I can't use the water. Sorry."

"That's okay. We could melt snow."

"I should. If the power stays out too long, I'm sure we'll get thirsty."

It would give him something to do.

Twenty minutes later he had a couple of pails heaped with snow sitting by the fireplace. "That won't give us much, but it'll be a start," he said. "Thankfully, my cell phone is still working. The power company said a line was down. Might be hours before the power comes on again."

He knew he should go into the study again. Call his family. Let them know what was going on.

Instead, he stood beside her, loathe to go back to his side of the couch, reluctant to leave, curious to see what she was doing.

"Do you mind if I ask what you're working on?" he said, resting his hands on the arm of the couch behind her, deliberately putting himself closer to her.

She shot a look up at him, her eyes glimmering in the half-light. "Just some plans. For the bakery."

"Can I have a look?"

Her slight hesitation made him wish he hadn't asked, but then she moved over to give him room and tilted the laptop toward him as he sat down. "These are the floor plans for the back end."

He looked at the two-dimensional schematics, not sure what to say.

"I can see you don't know what is what," she said with a chuckle.

"The only time I was in the back of a bakery was when I was with a friend. He had to pick up a cake for his mother. But that was a while back. That bakery is closed now. Has been for about six months."

"I saw an article about that in the paper. The one I used for the kids' hats," she said. "Are you saying there's no bakery at all in town anymore?"

"Oh, no. The co-op has one, but it's part of the store. Not the same as the old Chernowyk bakery. They had such fun and interesting pastries. At Christmas they had rows and rows of Christmas cookies you could mix and match."

"I noticed it was for sale," she said.

Her comment made him curious and, beneath that, he felt a tiny glimmer of hope.

He tried to shut his runaway thoughts down as he focused on the glare of the computer screen. "So you and Sally were going to run this?"

Adele nodded, her finger resting on the track pad, sending the cursor around the plans. "That was the initial plan, but Sally bowed out as soon as she was diagnosed six months ago. I found someone else willing to come on board."

Wyatt heard the hesitation in her voice. "You sound uncertain. Is that because you had planned to do this with Sally?"

Adele nodded, and in the glow of the computer screen, Wyatt caught the melancholy look on her face. "My partner is great, but I have to confess, I feel like I'm betraying Sally by moving on."

Wyatt heard the sorrow in her voice and realized that the death of her friend was yet another loss for her to deal with. A very recent loss at that.

"You must miss her," he said quietly, feeling yet again a tiny stab of guilt that he couldn't remember her better.

"I do. We got along great. She was an inspiration to me. I just wish..."

She paused, and Wyatt wanted to comfort her again. Hold her close. This woman brought out a protective side of him he'd never experienced with Theresa or anyone he dated before her. He doubted, however, that she would appreciate that. She had an independent streak that he'd already seen evidence of.

"Tell me about these plans," he said, shifting to a safer topic. Sally was someone he still struggled to deal with. Even though he knew she'd manipulated him, the fact that he'd been a willing partner and therefore, fully as guilty, haunted him.

It would take time to reconcile that.

"This is where I want to put the ovens," Adele said, pointing to the plans. "And this is where I'll put the cooling racks." She moved her cursor around, explaining what each part of the store would hold. Where she would put the walk-in fridge and freezer, the mixers, and how she would arrange the other tools to create a good workflow.

He had no clue about half of what she was talking about, but as she spoke, she grew animated. Excited.

This was an important dream to her, he realized.

"What kind of equipment were you hoping to purchase at the auction?" he asked.

"I can show you the listing," she said, clicking on an icon and opening a new web page.

She went to the auction site he had spent many an hour on looking for farm equipment.

She clicked and shifted, and a row of pictures flashed up. "Here's the fridge and freezer, the oven, and all the other equipment, like the mixer, dough divider, and the pans and decorating supplies.

"That seems like a lot of stuff."

"It is a lot." She bit her lip and Wyatt sensed some nervousness. "But I've been looking for a while, and this is the first time

I've seen enough equipment to get me started. Though..." She let the word drift off, shaking her head. As if she would say something, then caught herself.

"Looks like they've divided it up into three lots."

She nodded. "The fridge and freezer, the ovens and cooling racks, and then the miscellaneous other equipment." She sighed, leaning back as she studied the listing. "I'm not thrilled that they've done that, at all."

"Why?"

"I have no idea what each lot might go for. One might go cheap, the other too much. Leah and I need everything that's here to make a go of the bakery. I can't afford to buy what we need brand new."

"And when is this auction?"

She was quiet a moment, tapping her finger on her computer. "Saturday," she said finally.

Wyatt bit his lip, listening to the storm.

"What will happen if you can't make it?"

"I'm optimistic I can. But I talked to Leah and she said she would go if I couldn't make it. We'll stay in touch to check on how much she can bid."

But she frowned as she spoke.

"You seem concerned yet."

"I guess I'm a control freak. I had counted on going myself, but I have to trust her. We'll be partners, so I may as well start now."

Wyatt didn't blame her for being concerned. He would feel the same.

"Well, at least you'll be able to talk to each other during the auction," he assured her.

She nodded, but he could tell she was still uncertain. He just hoped the power outage wouldn't last too long. Who knew how that would affect the cell phone towers? So far, he still had reception.

"And what would you be baking in this bakery of yours?" he asked, hoping to distract her.

She perked up. "I've got some great ideas for some intriguing pastries I'd love to try."

She sounded so excited and animated, and it made Wyatt smile.

"I'm guessing you have a Pinterest board?" he asked.

Her surprised look made him laugh.

"Should I be worried that you know about Pinterest?"

"No. I don't have a board, but my sister, Carly, did for the events center she always wanted to start, and so did Theresa—" He paused, not so sure he should've brought his ex-wife's name into the conversation. Right now he wanted it to be about just him and Adele, the two of them sitting side by side in the dark. Connecting. Sharing.

Even as he formulated the thought, he realized that the very plans she was showing him were for a place she wanted to start in another city, far away from here.

Later, he told himself, clinging to the faint hope that had burned deep inside each time they had kissed. Each moment they spent together. He knew he had to be careful, but he also knew that in the short time he had spent with Adele, he'd discovered someone special. Someone loving, caring, and kind.

Someone he could—

"That's a lot of pastries," he said, slamming the door on thoughts he couldn't let wander too far, focusing on the pictures of the pastel-colored confections she had pulled up.

"I know we wouldn't be able to make all of them, but this is just for inspiration."

"I like the looks of that one," he said, pointing to a chocolate cake frosted with white icing, sprinkled with chocolate shavings. "Simple. Elegant, and chocolate."

"Sounds like you're a fan." She chuckled.

"Huge fan. Huge." He pointed to another picture. "I'm guessing that's supposed to be bread?"

"I want to try some artisan-type bread, and these ovens will make that easier," she said.

"Bread is bread, isn't it?"

"Hush your mouth. Never say that to a baker." She put her finger on his lips, smiling, her eyes glinting.

Wyatt couldn't stop himself. He caught her wrist then pressed a gentle kiss to the inside, his eyes still on hers.

"Really. What else should I never say to a baker?" he teased.

"That margarine is just as good as butter."

"It isn't?"

"No. Of course not." She looked almost indignant. "Butter gives everything a richer flavor. Margarine is made of oil and water, so—"

He stopped her flow of words with another kiss. Then another. She swept her free arm around his, pulling him close, holding him close, their mouths melding.

Her laptop fell to the floor with a clunk and Adele pulled back, her eyes wide.

Wyatt bent over to pick it up, handing it to her. "I hope it's okay."

"It's fallen before," she whispered, her fingers pressed against her mouth, as if unsure of what just happened.

Wyatt set the laptop aside, his hands holding her arms, unable to keep his eyes off her.

He wanted to ask her what was going on between them. What he dared expect. What she wanted.

But just then a small voice called out from the top of the stairs.

"Dean is thirsty, Daddy."

Maya.

A gentle reminder of his obligations.

"I can get it," Adele said, getting to her feet.

"No. I'll do it," he said, waving away her offer.

Adele sat down again, a curious expression on her face, as if realizing that this would be Wyatt's job from here on in.

He grabbed the flashlight and checked the snow in the pail. Thankfully enough was melted for at least one drink of water. And thankfully, it looked clean.

He took it up the stairs. Maya was crouched at the top of the stairs, her nightgown tucked around her upraised knees. "I told Dean he could ask you, but he didn't want to."

Wyatt felt a tiny twist of his heart at her words. "I'll take this to him," he said, flashlight in one hand and the glass of ice-cold water in the other.

They walked together to the bedroom. Dean was sitting up in the bed, his hands resting on either side of him.

"I'm sorry," he said.

Wyatt shook his head and brought the cup to him, sitting down on the edge of the bed, setting the flashlight on the bedside table. "You never have to apologize for asking for water," he said, giving him the glass. "Don't drink it too fast. It's really cold and you'll get brain freeze."

"Like when I eat ice cream?"

"Yes. Just like that," Wyatt said, smiling at the little guy.

Dean took a few careful drinks, then handed him the cup. "Maya said I could ask, but I was afraid."

"Of what?"

"That you would be mad."

"I wouldn't be mad." That Dean would think that hurt him somehow. He turned to his daughters, who were both awake now, watching him, their eyes gleaming in the half-dark. "Have I ever been mad at you for asking for a drink?"

They shook their heads. "Daddy always gets a drink for us," Maya put in, looking at Dean.

"And if you ask, I'll always get one for you," he said to Dean.

"But not four drinks," Maria said. "Four is too many."

Wyatt had to chuckle at that. "Yes. Four is too many drinks."

"I won't ask for that many," Dean assured him, looking so earnest it almost broke Wyatt's heart.

He moved closer and stroked the boy's hair. "I know you won't. You're a great little guy."

Dean's smile wound its way into his heart. Wyatt gave in to an impulse and pulled him close, hugging him. "I'm glad you're here," Wyatt said, laying his head on his son's.

Dean wrapped his arms around Wyatt and snuggled in, so easily accepting the affection Wyatt was giving him. As he did, Wyatt felt a protective and surprising wave of love wash over him. And with that came a sense of relief that he could feel this way about a complete stranger. Yet he knew, on some level, he felt a connection to this boy that could not be explained other than biology.

"I like it here too," Dean said when they pulled apart.

"We hug too," Maya called out.

Wyatt chuckled, then went over to his daughters and gave them each a tight hug.

"Okay, now it's time to sleep," he said, picking up the flashlight but leaving the cup behind.

They didn't complain about the dark and settled down. "Good night, you kiddos," Wyatt said. He walked out of the room but stayed just outside the door, listening. He waited till they were quiet, then he walked back downstairs.

Adele was packing up her computer when he came down, her face hidden from the glow of the fire.

"You quitting for the night?"

"My battery is running low. I don't want to drain it, and the internet is down so..."

He should let her go. He should take the out she was giving him. But the emotions between them were real. He knew that deep in his soul.

And he sensed that she felt the same.

CAROLYNE AARSEN

He couldn't carry on this way.

"We need to talk," he said, keeping his voice quiet.

She clutched her laptop, looking down. Then, to his surprise, she nodded and sat back down on the couch.

Could he do this?

He thought back to Theresa. How back and forth their relationship had been. He thought of Sally, and shame slithered through him. Which made what he had to say to Adele even more important.

He dropped onto the couch beside her, leaning forward, his hands clasped as if he didn't trust himself not to touch her. To pull her close. To express the connection they shared.

"And where do we go from here?" he asked, deciding to head straight to the point.

"We being you and us?" she asked.

"Yes."

He didn't trust himself to look at her. Instead he focused on the flickering flames ahead of him, the warmth they created, the soft hiss of sap burning out of the logs.

"I'm not sure."

That didn't give him much to go on, but he understood her hesitancy. Just a few moments ago they were discussing her plans for her future.

Away from here.

"I know that I'm attracted to you," he said, finally shooting her a quick glance. "And I don't think it's simple loneliness. I've dated other women after Theresa left but never felt anything for them like I feel for you."

Adele wasn't looking at him, her hands clasped in her lap.

"But I have my kids to think about. Three kids, now. I've always tried to be careful whenever I dated anyone, but our situation is, well, unique." He gave her a careful smile, hoping it would ease any discomfort his comment might cause her.

She returned his smile, leaning back on the couch, keeping her distance.

"That about sums it up." He held her gaze, wishing he knew what else to say.

"And just a few moments ago you got a glimpse of my hopes for my future," she said. "And it doesn't mesh with your situation."

"I'm not asking for any kind of—"

"I know," she said, holding her hand up. "The only thing you've asked me for is to help you. And I feel like we're on the edge of something that could go in either direction. I'm not going to lie, I'm scared."

"Of what?"

"I've lost so much in my life. I can't...I can't..." She pressed her hand against her chest, as if holding in her heart.

"I know what you mean," he said, keeping his voice quiet. Unthreatening. "I would be lying if I said I wasn't afraid too. But I also know that you're a wonderful, loving person. I feel like I can trust you." He released a short laugh. "In fact, I've already had to trust you in so many ways."

"That means so much to me," she whispered.

They were both silent a moment as their gazes meshed, each seeming to delve into the other.

"And right now we can't get away from each other because, well, storm," he said, waving his hand toward the darkened windows. "So we'll have to figure out how we go on."

"Carefully?" she asked, her voice hesitant.

He knew it wasn't realistic or practical to expect anything else from her, but he was thankful she was still willing to move on.

"I think that's a good idea."

What shape that would take he wasn't sure, but for now, this was enough.

CHAPTER TWELVE

*A*dele sat on her bed, her flashlight sitting on the table beside it, sending a cone of light into the room and out the open door. The heat of the fireplace couldn't quite keep the rooms upstairs as warm as the ones downstairs, but she was comfortable enough if she kept the door open.

It was too early to go to bed, but after she and Wyatt talked, she knew she needed to retreat, regroup, and think.

Pray?

For a moment Adele wished she had the Bible her foster parents had given her. She had left it behind in her apartment in Whitehorse. She hadn't read it for ages.

But now, she wished she had it.

Her mind ticked over the conversation she and Wyatt had. Wondered what she was allowed to think. Allowed to feel.

She knew they were attracted to each other. She also knew that, as Wyatt said, they had to be careful. But she knew that while she was with him, she felt a sense of rightness, of completeness, she had never felt before. That had to mean something, right?

But where did she go from here?

She thought of the paper still tucked in the pocket of her blue jeans.

You can't abandon your plans now. You can't abandon Leah now.

But could she walk away from Wyatt? From Dean?

It was at this moment that she missed Sally the most. Sally had been her sounding board. The person who could always look at the bigger picture. Look at things in their proper perspective. Even as she lay dying, she was giving Adele advice on how to run the bakery, how to set things up.

Encouraging her to go to church, read her Bible. Pray.

Adele pressed her hands to her eyes, wishing she could stop her roiling and confused thoughts.

She took a breath and looked heavenward, as if waiting for some sign.

I don't know what to do, Lord, she finally prayed. It was all she could manage.

And yet, as she and Wyatt laid things out just a few moments ago, she felt as if he, more than anyone, understood her fears. Acknowledged them.

Trust in the Lord and lean not on your own understanding. In all your ways acknowledge Him and He will make straight your path.

The verse slipped into her mind, and despite her own confusion, it made her smile. It was a verse that Bonnie had printed out and framed and hung in Adele's bedroom. The verse had comforted her many times when she wasn't sure of where her life would go.

And now, it seemed to show her what she needed to do. Rather than try to figure everything out, to solve all the problems, she needed to trust. To release control. She felt a momentary clutch of panic. She couldn't do that. Not yet.

So she picked up her phone, glanced at the time and how much power she had. Thankfully enough.

She dialed Leah's number.

"Hey, everything okay?" Leah sounded breathless.

"Um. Yeah."

"I was just packing for my trip to Edmonton. I decided to leave tomorrow morning first thing. That gives me a chance to check things out before the auction on Saturday. I won't be as rushed."

"That should give you more than enough time, but yeah. Good idea."

Leah was quiet a moment.

"Are you okay?" Adele asked.

"Yeah. I'm fine. Excited. Nervous. But this will be cool. I'm still thrilled that you're willing to take me on board. This is something I've wanted to do for a long time." She released a sigh. "Sorry. I know this happened because of Sally but still—"

"Don't worry about it," Adele assured her. "I know Sally was pleased I managed to find you."

"So, what did you want?"

"To check in. Touch base. We haven't talked for a while."

"I know. How are things going with Dean and...and his father?"

"Good. Now. I think it'll all work out."

"And you? Are you okay with leaving him behind?"

No. I'm not okay at all. But he's not my child, and this is a better place.

"He's with his father. Kids need to be with family," she said.

"I know. I understand."

Adele heard the sincerity in her voice and knew that Leah spoke from personal experience. She and her brother had been adopted as children when Leah was four and her brother one. Leah had, of late, been wondering about her biological parents. Her adoptive parents were still alive, and she was afraid they'd feel betrayed if she asked them about it. So she had kept her questions to herself.

"I was wondering about this equipment," Adele continued. "I noticed that they split it into three lots. I didn't expect that."

"Me neither, and I'm worried about that."

Adele clutched the phone, Leah's concern giving her a tiny opening.

"What do you think we should do if it goes too high?"

"It won't. I can't see that too many people would be interested."

"You just need one more person to push the price up." Adele blew out a sigh.

Silence followed Adele's comment. Then, "What are you trying to say? You sound uncertain. Are you backing out?"

The harsh tone in Leah's voice made Adele wonder if she'd pushed a bit too hard.

"No. I'm not," she hastened to assure her. "I still really want to do this."

"I sense a hesitancy though."

Adele pulled in a deep breath and sent up a quick prayer. "I found another possibility," she said. "A fully stocked bakery with all the equipment."

"But not in Whitehorse."

"No. Here. In Millar's Crossing."

Leah was quiet again, and the silence sprawled between them, growing heavier with each second.

"Is it because of Dean that you're considering this?"

Adele had to weigh that question. She could hide behind that. It would make it easier, but at the same time part of her needed to talk to someone. Anyone.

"I met someone."

"In Millar's Crossing? How?"

"Dean's father."

"Oh."

That single word shivered over the line, and Adele felt as if she had stepped out into the space she'd tried to keep between herself and Wyatt.

"I'm not sure what's happening, but I feel like I know this guy. I feel like there's a chance between us."

"And if it doesn't happen? Would you still be willing to stay in Millar's Crossing?"

Adele held that question, thinking, weighing.

"There's still Dean." Though would she be able to stay if things didn't work out between them? Wyatt had found a place in her heart that had been unoccupied before. Every minute she spent with him created a stronger connection. She knew she was on the cusp of something special. Wonderful.

"That's true." Leah sighed. "Well, we have a few days yet to figure things out. I don't know if I'm ready to ditch Whitehorse. Though lately, Chris..." She let the last word ease away.

Leah wasn't one to say a lot about her personal life, but Adele had heard stories through the Whitehorse grapevine about Leah's brother, Chris. How Leah had bailed him out time after time. "He just got a job in Edmonton, so I'm hoping he'll settle down."

Adele had to fight down the urge to give Leah advice. But she and Leah weren't that close, so she kept her comments to herself.

"Anyhow, I'll think about this. Meantime, I'm still heading to Edmonton for the auction. I should tell you, they changed the listing. They moved the first items to Thursday evening, the second batches to first thing Friday morning."

Panic shivered through her. This was sooner than she had figured on.

"I'm still snowed in, so I'm not sure I'll be able to make it," she said. "Otherwise, we'll go with our other plan of me staying in touch with you on the phone while you bid." She had to trust that she and Leah could stay connected. That Leah would make the right choices.

"Not ideal, but we can work around this. I would prefer it if you could be there. In the meantime, stay safe."

Adele said good-bye and then pulled in a long breath. Nothing had been decided. Nothing was definite.

But she felt as if she had opened up another option.

An option for staying.

The lights flicked on, the refrigerator started humming, and Wyatt sat bolt upright in his bed, blinking, realizing he forgot to turn the room's lights off when he went to bed.

He checked the time on his phone. Ten-thirty. He pulled on some clothes and stepped out into the family room, walking around and turning all the lights off. He went upstairs. It was dark and he could hear the kids' deep breathing. Adele's room was also dark, so he returned downstairs again.

He plugged his phone in and sat on the edge of his bed, wondering if he dared phone his brothers and Carly at this time of night.

It had to happen soon. It wasn't right to keep them in the dark about Dean.

Start with Reuben, he told himself. Last he heard, his brother was in B.C., which was an hour behind. He pulled in a deep breath, sent up a prayer, and punched in Reuben's number. His brother answered on the third ring.

"Hey. What's up?" Reuben asked, sounding puzzled. "Everything okay?"

"Yeah. I guess."

"You guess? What's going on?" Trust Reuben to get straight to the point. "You never call me more than once a month."

Wyatt sat back on the bed, his legs stretched out in front of him, trying to find the right words.

"Remember that trip we made to Mexico?"

"After Theresa dumped you? Again?"

"That one."

"Vaguely."

Wyatt felt a flicker of shame at what he had to say next. "Apparently I hooked up with a woman there. Told me her name was Jane."

A moment of silence followed his comment.

Wyatt plunged on. "And, apparently, I got Jane pregnant."

"What?"

His brother's question exploded in his ear, and Wyatt closed his eyes, breathing, praying for strength.

"Seriously?" Reuben continued.

"I wouldn't joke about something like this."

"How did you find out? When did you find out?"

"Last week Monday, except I didn't know for sure until Sunday."

"And you decide to tell me now?"

Wyatt bristled at the veiled condemnation in his brother's voice. "I wasn't sure until I got the DNA test results back. And then we got socked in by a storm that knocked the power out."

Another beat of silence. "I'm guessing the DNA test was positive."

"Ninety-nine and a whole bunch of nines after that positive."

"Whoa. That's kind of overwhelming. I'm stunned."

"You're not the only one."

"Why did you find out just now? That was almost six years ago."

"His mother passed away. Asked a friend to bring Dean, my son, here."

"A boy."

"Yep."

"And his mother is dead?"

"Yes." He took a breath, then filled his brother in on all the other details. Why Sally or Jane had kept it a secret. Why she had waited this long. All the while Wyatt spoke, his mind shifted to Adele. He kept her out of the conversation. For now, Dean was a reality.

Adele, he wasn't sure of. Nor did he want to bring their relationship out. Not yet. Things were too new. Too fresh.

Too uncertain.

But even as he thought that, he felt a sense of rightness that he had never felt with anyone before.

And that had to count for something.

"So when are you coming back?" Wyatt asked, dealing with the other reality of his life.

"I hope to be coming back around spring. This job will be over then, and I'll be ready to get back to Millar's Crossing."

Wyatt didn't want to tell him that Katrina had moved back as well. No sense rocking that particular boat. Besides, Reuben had been happily married to Denise. Had deeply grieved her death.

He probably didn't think much about his ex-girlfriend.

"Okay. Good. That'll work out. We'll need to do a bunch of fencing."

Their conversation slipped to the ranch, their plans for expansion. How Finn and Carly were doing.

Wyatt knew he needed to talk to them too some time or other.

But as he and Reuben chatted, as he skated around the reality of the woman in the house who now held his heart, he knew that sooner or later he would have to face what was going on between them.

Thank goodness the waterers hadn't frozen while the power was out.

And thank goodness the storm had quit.

The sun was just coming up on the horizon, promising a beautiful day, as Wyatt made his way back to the house across the snow-covered yard. The temperature had risen overnight, and the wind had died down.

Lights were on in the house and smoke curled up from the chimney, rising straight up into the air.

Adele was probably up already. Making coffee, getting breakfast together.

He paused, his mind sifting back to the conversation he and Adele had last night. He had to be careful, but even while his practical self laid out all the reasons, his heart couldn't stop the gentle lift that thoughts of Adele created.

She was kind, caring, loving.

And she knew how to run a tractor.

He smiled at that last thought, trying to imagine Theresa coming anywhere near anything that had an internal combustion engine. The picture didn't gel and as he trudged through the snow, he caught a shadow in the kitchen's window.

And any thought of Theresa fled.

He wanted nothing more than to go straight into the house, talk to Adele, connect with her. See where things would be going.

But first, he had to shovel the sidewalk. Again.

He was about to grab the shovel when his cell phone rang. He tugged his gloves off and dug past his coat to pull the phone out of his shirt pocket. He glanced at the screen. The clinic.

Then he remembered. Ruby had talked about setting up an appointment for the twins. He hadn't checked the calendar for a couple of days, but he remembered seeing it.

He took the call and thanked the receptionist for the reminder telling her that yes, he would be there tomorrow. He wondered if he dared ask Adele to come along. They could go out for lunch afterwards.

He held the thought, then, just as he was about to put the phone back in his pocket it rang again.

Oh, brother, he thought. *The snow stops falling and everyone wants to reach out.*

This time it was Ruby Mulder. He felt a niggle of guilt. He'd forgotten about their nanny.

"Hey, Ruby," he said. "How are things going? How is your mother?"

"Good. Great, in fact," Ruby said, sounding exuberant. "My mom is doing well, thanks for asking, and I'm happy to tell you I can come back sooner than I expected. I'll be in Millar's Crossing day after tomorrow, if that works out for you."

He should be happy about this. Two weeks ago, he would have been thrilled.

But now?

Ruby coming back would change everything. Adele would have one less reason to stay.

"Okay. That should work out well."

"Are you sure? Or did you find someone else?"

She must have heard the faint displeasure in his voice.

"No. No. It's fine. I've got someone here for the next few days, so just come when it works."

"Okay. I'll see you later then."

Wyatt ended the call and shoved the phone in his coat pocket. Well, things were moving along.

He knew his and Adele's little idyll couldn't last forever. Knew that eventually the outside world would come barging in.

He just wished it wouldn't happen so soon. Before they had a chance to find their way through this relationship.

Fifteen minutes later he had the snow shoveled off the walk and most of the snow brushed off Adele's car. It had gotten buried during the snowstorm. He found the cord for the block heater and reminded himself to bring an extension cord back next time he went to the shop.

He strode up the now-clean sidewalk to the house, his enthusiasm for seeing Adele again quickening his steps.

He opened the door with a smile that was immediately dissolved by the cacophony of sorrow that greeted him. With quick movements he shed his boots and coat, hurrying inside to see what had happened.

Adele sat by the table, holding the twins leaning against her, sobbing uncontrollably. Dean had his head on the table, crying as well.

"What's happening?" Wyatt asked, walking over to Dean and crouching down beside him.

"We miss our mommy," Maya howled.

Wyatt wasn't sure where that came from. The girls were six months old when Theresa left them all.

"I want my mommy," Maria put in, echoing her sister, as always following her lead.

He shot Adele a questioning look. She angled her chin toward Dean who was sniffing, his shoulders shaking. "He misses Sally," she said, above the sound of the girls' crying. "I think the girls picked up on that."

Wyatt stroked Dean's back, feeling sorry for the little guy. Then he gave into an impulse and pulled him into his arms, cradling his head on his shoulder as he sat on a chair beside him.

To his surprise, Dean burrowed into his neck, his arms clinging to him. "My mommy is dead," he whispered, as if unable to articulate his sorrow.

"I'm sorry, buddy," he said, holding him just a little closer. He wasn't sure how else to assure him. Though he was much older than Dean was when his mother died, he knew how much he resented people telling him he would get over it. That she was in a better place.

Though both comments were intrinsically true, they were cold comfort to a child grieving the loss of his mother.

"It's hard, isn't it?" he asked, resting his head on Dean's, feeling a surprising surge of protective love. He wanted to take away his sorrow, to make it easy for him, but he knew from his own experience that grief had to find its own way of working itself out.

Though he couldn't figure out why the girls were so upset. They hadn't known their mother at all.

Finally the girls quieted down and Adele stood, settling them on the chairs. She took the tissue box from the top of the refrigerator and brought it back to the table. Snagging a couple out she wiped the girls' eyes and noses, then pushed the box closer to Wyatt.

She wasn't looking at him, and the serious look on her face created a wink of concern.

He waited until Dean lifted his head from his shoulder then handed him a tissue as well. Dean sniffed, looking at Wyatt, blinking the remnants of his tears away.

Then he gave him a wavering smile that dove straight into Wyatt's heart. Wyatt hugged him again. Hard. Tight. Then he let Dean slip off his lap. Dean headed right to the girls, who now sat quietly in their chairs.

He gave them each a hug, and patted their backs. "You'll be okay," he assured them.

The sight made Wyatt love the little guy even more.

"Your mommy is happy in heaven," Dean said, his tone solemn. "Just like mine is."

Maria frowned at that, her tears now gone. "Our mommy isn't in heaven. She's in California."

"Here's some milk and cookies for you sad little kids," Adele said, distracting Dean from the questions Wyatt could see in his expression.

"I love cookies," Maya announced, obviously over her bout of sorrow. "Do you love cookies, Dean?"

He nodded and sat down, taking a huge drink of his milk. He pulled in a long breath, as if settling his own emotions, then looked up at Adele. "My mommy is in heaven, isn't she?"

Adele nodded, stroking his hair in a tender gesture, the affection on her face showing Wyatt how she loved this little boy.

Could she still be considering leaving?

"I'm making some coffee. Did you want some?" Adele asked Wyatt, returning to the counter, her back to him as she plugged in the kettle.

"I'd love some. But I can make it."

"No. Just stay there. I'm fine." She sounded distracted.

He sat back, watching as she bustled about the kitchen, cleaning, wiping, avoiding him.

He wanted to ask what was going on, but not in front of the kids who were gulping down their milk and munching on cookies. Obviously feeling better.

"We go play pirate," Maya announced when she was done.

Maria, of course, agreed, and Dean went along as well.

They went downstairs and he and Adele were alone.

She brought the French press and two mugs and sat down across from him.

He poured her a cup then one for himself, leaning his elbows on the table, watching her, willing her to look at him. Give him some indication of what was going on behind those shuttered eyes.

"Is everything okay?" He was struggling with his own second thoughts and concerns. He needed to know where she was at.

It was as if they were both hesitating, waiting to see which way the other would jump. Who would make which move?

"Yeah. Just lots of things on my mind."

He could relate.

"I just got a couple of phone calls," he said, trying for ordinary. "I have to take the twins into town tomorrow. Doctor's appointment."

"Just a routine checkup?"

"Yeah. It's at eleven."

"Did you want me to stay behind with Dean?"

"No. I thought I would take him along."

"Okay. That should work. I have to head to town anyway. Have a few things I need to do."

She sounded mysterious, and he wasn't sure he wanted to know what she had to do in town, but it wasn't his place to ask.

"We could meet for lunch," she said, giving him a careful smile.

The tension holding his shoulders eased, and he returned her smile. "That would be great. It'll be nice to get out and see other humans."

He didn't want to think of what the implications of being seen together could mean, but right now, holding Adele's gaze, feeling the warmth of her smile, he didn't care.

The sound of feet hammering up the stairs broke into the moment, and the kids were back.

"Can we go sliding?" Dean asked as they joined Adele and Wyatt at the table.

"Sure," Wyatt said with a grin. "I think that's a great idea."

"Will you come?" Dean asked Adele.

"Of course I will. It'll be good for all of us to get out of the house."

Her eyes met Wyatt's, and they shared another smile.

"I think we could pull you guys around on the snow machine," Wyatt suggested. "It's gorgeous out and there's lots of snow."

"Yay. Skidoo," Maria yelled, jumping up and down.

"What's a skidoo?" Dean asked, frowning, unsure.

"Come outside and we'll show you," Wyatt said, getting up from the table.

Half an hour later the kids were all bundled up, the sleds were tied up behind the snow sled and the kids were climbing on.

"Aren't you coming?" Wyatt called out above the noise of the engine as Adele stood aside. "You can ride on the snow machine and watch the kids."

She hesitated, but only for a moment. Plowing through the snow, she made her way to the snow machine and got on behind him. "Let me know if the kids fall off, okay?" he said, grinning at her.

Her toque was pulled low over her head, her hair pulled back and tucked in her jacket. Her cheeks were already pink from the outside air and her eyes shone. He gunned the engine, the motor engaged, and they were off. He took it slow, making sure the kids were okay.

The kids were squealing, laughing their pleasure as the sleds they were on plowed through the snow. Wyatt glanced back from time to time, his gaze flicking from the kids to Adele. She was laughing as much as the kids were.

"This is great," she called out, hanging on to the back bar of the sled. "I've never ridden on a snow machine before."

"Faster, Daddy, faster," Maya called out, her toque askew, her hands wrapped around her sister. Dean was on the other sled, and his grin was wide with pleasure.

"Should I go faster, Dean?" he called out, wanting to make sure the little boy was okay.

Dean nodded, holding his thumb up.

So Wyatt pressed on the throttle and they went faster. He made a wide turn in the field, and then he heard a scream.

"The girls just fell off the sled," Adele cried, grabbing his arm. She sounded frightened, but when Wyatt looked back, he saw the girls lying in the snow, kicking their feet.

"We'll loop round to pick them up." He knew they were okay. They couldn't hurt themselves falling into this much snow.

When they got to them, the girls were struggling to get to their feet, laughing. Wyatt jumped off the snow machine and waded through the snow to help them onto the sled. Adele was right behind him, still concerned.

"You girls okay?" she asked, pulling Maria to her feet.

"That was fun," Maria said, snow crusting her face and toque. "Do it again."

"Should we keep going?" Wyatt asked, brushing the snow off Maya.

"Yes. Go again," she called out. "Adele, you come with us."

"No. That's okay," Adele said.

"You chicken?" Wyatt teased.

"Of course not. Someone needs to ride shotgun." She gave him a playful shove.

He took a step back and lost his balance, falling backward into the snow.

"I'm sorry," she said, hands on her mouth, looking shocked. "I was just teasing."

"Yeah. Sure," he returned, tugging on his gloves as she held her hand out to help him up. He took her hand and instead of pulling himself to his feet, he pulled her down into the snow. "Sorry," he said, grinning. "Just teasing."

"Whoa, no fair," she called out. But she was laughing as she struggled to get to her feet. Now it was his turn to help her out, and she returned the favor, pulling him down too.

The kids joined in, piling on, screaming their joy.

Snow slithered down Wyatt's neck as he play wrestled with the kids in the deep snow. Dean joined in and then, so did Adele.

It was a tangle of arms and legs and laughter all around.

One moment Adele landed on top of Wyatt, their faces inches from each other, emotions sparking between them so intense he was surprised the snow on their faces didn't melt. He had to resist the urge to kiss her, and from the way her eyes held his, he guessed she felt the same. Instead he brushed the snow off her, his hands gentle.

"Get up, get up," Maria called out, pulling on their arms. "Go sledding."

"Duty calls," Wyatt said, struggling to his feet and helping Adele up as well. He gave her a quick, one-armed hug. She leaned into him for a moment and then they got the kids back on the sleds.

A few moments later they were on their way. Adele sat backwards to watch the kids, but she leaned against his back, her hand behind her, resting on his leg.

This was right. This was good.

And as they made another loop around the field, he felt like things had shifted to a place of no return.

CHAPTER THIRTEEN

"The kids are hopefully down for the night," Wyatt announced as he dropped onto the couch. Far enough from Adele to keep the distance they had spoken of yesterday, yet close enough that if she wanted, she could reach out and touch him.

"I would hope so, after spending that much time outside."

"It was good for them. I'm glad we could do that."

Adele caught his grin as she remembered that moment in the snow. Though they hadn't kissed, she had felt as if they had.

"Me too," she said. "Though I had to change my shirt, I got so much snow down my coat."

"Serves you right for pushing me around like that."

"Just asserting myself."

"And I'm asserting myself and asking you to come and sit closer to me," he said, grinning at her.

"Bully," she said, but she moved up beside him, snuggling up against him.

"I know we said we should be careful, but I'm thinking things are moving in a good direction. Am I right?"

She was quiet, thinking of the shift in plans she was contemplating.

Though part of her tried to tell herself it was for Dean, it was for herself and Wyatt as well.

"You're right," she said, resting her head on his shoulder, her arm twined through his. Though she wanted to kiss him, right now this felt even better. His hand stroked hers, making gentle circles on her skin.

And as they sat there, just touching, she realized that she missed this connection even more than the more sensual kiss. This ordinary being together. A connection, a peaceful bonding.

"This might seem odd, but I feel like I shouldn't be staying here at the ranch. Now that the roads are cleared."

He was quiet a moment, then she could feel his chuckle. "I think you're right. And with Ruby coming back, it might look better."

"I just don't want to create gossip," she said.

"So you'll be leaving tomorrow?"

"Actually, I'm going tonight." Adele was reluctant to leave. She knew the sooner she left, the better it would look for everyone. "I've got my stuff packed up."

"And then?"

He threw the words out casually, but she knew where he was going. Could feel the tension in the arm curled around her.

"I'm sticking around. For a while." She tacked on the last words as a gentle out. A way of evading a complete commitment that frightened her even as it appealed. It was a delicate tightrope she was walking. Letting Wyatt know she was open to whatever may happen, yet giving herself space. Old fears still haunted her.

They made her need to be the one in control of the leaving.

"Okay. I don't like the idea of you traveling in the dark, but I can see your point." He seemed to relax as he spoke.

She was glad about his cooperation. She'd been reluctant to tell him, but she knew it would be for the best.

"You'll be leaving Dean here though, right?" His quiet question held a leaden weight.

Adele realized the import of the situation. She had come here with Dean for that very reason. To leave him here. But now that she was moving out, it felt so final.

"Of course," she said. "This is his home. I explained things to him this afternoon. He was unhappy. I think that's why he was crying about missing his mom, but afterward he realized that this is where he'll be staying."

"He's such a sweet kid," Wyatt said. "Sally did a good job with him. I wish...I wish I could have known her despite our first meeting."

The mention of her friend's name created another flicker of sorrow. "I wish you could have too. She grew up a lot after Dean was born. Or so she tells me."

"Anyway, I hope he's okay," Wyatt said. "I'm sure he'll have some sad times, but he won't be alone."

An unspoken question hovered under Wyatt's words.

Would Adele be here?

"I'm sure he will too," Adele said, her heart still pierced at Dean's sorrow. But even as she spoke, she thought of the girls. "What about Maya and Maria? They also seemed pretty upset about their mother."

Wyatt eased out a sigh. "I don't know why. They were six months old when Theresa left. They don't remember her."

"Oh. From the way they were crying I thought they genuinely missed her."

"I have a feeling they were picking up on Dean's sadness. Figured they may as well join in. Not that I want to belittle or demean their tears, but they haven't seen Theresa since she left and have never cried about her before."

This surprised Adele. "Not at all?"

Wyatt's hand tensed on hers, tightened its grip, betraying his emotion. "Not at all. She just walked away without a fight."

"She didn't want custody?"

"Nope."

The single word had a harsh undertone of anger.

She wasn't sure what to say.

"Sorry. Didn't mean to bring in old history," Wyatt said after a heavy silence.

"That's so sad. She's missing out on a lot." Adele felt a surge of sympathy for Wyatt and the girls. To have been so completely abandoned. "She hasn't had any contact?"

He was quiet a moment, his eyes taking on a faraway look. "I shouldn't say any contact at all. I got an e-mail from her a while back saying that she'd made a mistake and that she wanted to see the girls. I was reluctant but figured it wasn't right of me to keep Maya and Maria from her, so I said I would arrange something that would work for her. I never heard from her again."

"I'm sorry to hear that."

"Well, I'm sorry to be talking about her." He shifted, lifting her face to his, stroking her cheek with his thumb. "I'd sooner talk about you and me."

"And I'd sooner talk about you," she returned, smiling.

"Boring subject." His expression shifted, and she saw the invitation in his eyes. She leaned in, and as their lips met, all thoughts of other people fled.

It was just she and Wyatt and the connection that grew deeper, stronger, each moment they spent together.

This was real. She knew it in her heart.

And as she nestled her head in his neck, catching her breath, her heart pounding, she also knew that she had to make a decision.

"So I'll meet you at Beef'n Such?" Wyatt asked. "It's just a burger place, but I figure it'll do."

Adele had come early this morning in time to help with breakfast. Dean wasn't even up so he hadn't been aware she was gone.

At breakfast he was his usual cheerful self, which eased her concerns.

"I'll be there," Adele said, zipping up Maria's jacket, touching her finger on the little girl's nose. Maria launched herself at Adele, giving her a tight hug. "You come with us," she announced.

"Don't worry, muffin, I'll see you for lunch." She held Maria by the arms, grinning at the little girl.

Seriously, she was so adorable.

She kept thinking about Theresa. Wondered how a mother could just walk away from her children. Dean wasn't even her own son, and it was hard enough to even think about leaving.

Her heart beat with a mixture of hope and anticipation as she straightened Maria's toque and tied her scarf. She was meeting the real estate agent this afternoon. So far no one else had expressed any interest in the building and the bakery equipment. Adele guessed it was because the owner wanted to sell it as an intact business, which would scare away many potential buyers.

"So, I'll see you later," Wyatt said, a faint question in his voice. As if he sensed she might bail on him. She wanted to reassure him. To tell him her plans, but she hesitated, allowing herself the tiny space she needed.

"For sure. I'm looking forward to trying those burgers you keep raving about."

"Best burgers for a hundred miles," he assured her. "Let's go, kiddos," he said, reaching out to take Maya and Maria's hands.

Dean trailed along behind, glancing back at Adele, a question in his eyes. Since they'd arrived, this was the first time he was going somewhere without her, and she read the concern on his face.

"I'll see you later," she assured him, giving him a quick hug.

He smiled then followed Wyatt and the girls, who were skipping alongside him, happy to be getting off the yard.

Adele watched them go, trying not to feel as if they were leaving her behind.

She shook off the emotion, then went back into the house.

She waited until Wyatt drove away before she called Leah.

"So, any thoughts about what we talked about the other night?" she asked, trying not to sound too breathless.

"Yeah. Lots of them. I just wish we didn't have to do this two days before the auction. It's fantastic equipment that's getting sold. From what I can see better and newer than the stuff in the bakery you showed me."

"But it could also mean we might lose out if we can't bid high enough," Adele said, injecting a practical note into the discussion, trying to be impartial. She didn't want to influence Leah.

But it was a very real scenario they had to take into consideration.

"We always knew that," Leah said.

"True. Which is why it would be a good idea to check this place out. If you're willing to think about Millar's Crossing."

Leah sighed, and Adele knew she was only doing this to humor her.

But once she caught sight of the mountains, saw the town, Adele hoped her friend would be convinced.

"I'm leaving right now to talk to the real estate agent and to hopefully check out the property." Adele had texted him this morning when Wyatt was out checking the cows and he immediately replied that he had time late this morning. So she set up an appointment.

"I can't get there in time to be with you, but take pictures and send them to me," Leah said. "I'd like to see what it looks like."

Adele didn't know if she was projecting her own vague hopes onto her friend, but she sensed that Leah was more open to the idea than previously.

"For sure I'll do that."

"Okay. I gotta go. Talk to you later." Leah hung up, and Adele held the phone, hoping, wondering if she dared to dream too far ahead. She'd had so many disappointments.

Help me trust, Lord. That no matter what happens, I'll be okay.

There was a lot riding on this moment, on her decisions. A commitment that frightened her.

But oh, the possibilities.

CHAPTER FOURTEEN

"I don't know enough about bakery equipment, but according to Lionel Chernowyk, the previous owner, it's all in good shape. The ovens are fairly new." Zachary Dover, the real estate agent, walked over to the ovens, as if to check out that fact.

Adele stood in the middle of the back room of the bakery, looking around, assessing, trying to imagine herself working here.

An apron hung on a hook on the butcher-block table. The counter held a few bowls and scrapers that hadn't been put away. The place looked like the previous owner had suddenly quit and not bothered to come back to tidy up. Adele was rather surprised. "Doesn't look like the Chernowyks were too concerned about how the place showed," she said, walking around the counters, checking the utensil rack. At least here, everything looked orderly. Spoons, spatulas, pastry brushes, whisks, and more all hung from hooks on a stainless-steel backing. Triple sink, overhead hose.

She smiled at the large plastic stacking container filled with cake decorating supplies. She wanted to dig in and see what tips were stocked there.

Focus on the big picture, she reminded herself.

"What do you think?" Zachary asked, hovering while trying not to look like he was hovering.

"It's been on the market for how long?"

"It's been vacant for six months, but I put it up a week or so ago. The bakery was part of a divorce settlement and, well, the couple couldn't agree on what to do with it. That's why it took so long to list."

Divorce. Split. Brokenness.

Adele tried not to let the words seep too deeply into her mind. The last few days she'd felt as if she had learned to trust more.

Her thoughts slipped to Wyatt. Again. He had gone through hard times, and yet he still seemed willing to be with her. She knew if she let this all go, she would regret it.

But did she dare open her heart again?

"And all this comes with?" she asked, checking out the ovens, the large walk-in fridge and freezer, burying her concerns.

"Yes. It's a turnkey operation."

Which made it even more appealing. She went to the front of the bakery, trying not to be too critical. Trying to see what she could do to spruce up the front end. Rough wooden shelves sagged along one wall. The display cases were in good shape but needed a good cleaning. The front desk could be replaced. And the flooring. Oh, my goodness. Curling and broken rubber tiles in a garish red and black. But it was the worn-out flooring in front of the display cases that made her smile. People stopping in had spent a lot of time standing there looking, thinking, choosing.

"Would I be able to be in contact with the owner?" she asked, shivering in the draft that seeped under the front door. Something that would also need to be replaced.

She was hoping she might purchase any of their recipes. She had her own, but if there were any popular items they'd made that the people here would request, she wanted to supply them.

"Of course. Lionel said he would talk with any potential owner. But only serious buyers. Not, as he said, lookie loos."

"And the financials?"

"I can supply those as well. I have to say, they look good. The Chernowyks did a steady business and were popular."

So far things sounded good. Almost too good.

"We can go to the office and I can go over them with you."

Adele meandered around the back room again, took several pictures for Leah, then joined Zachary. "Is the building leased or owned?"

"Owned. So that would be part of the purchase price."

That would make it more money upfront. She and Leah were leasing a building in Whitehorse. But owning the building would give them more leeway to renovate. More autonomy.

"And what is the asking price?"

"Like I said, we can talk about this at the office. I can give you more information."

Adele glanced at her watch. She had to pick up some groceries yet and drop them off at the Airbnb where she was able to stay again. She needed to send the photos to Leah and then join Wyatt and the kids for lunch.

"Not this time," she said, giving him a smile. "I have a business partner. I want to start with the biggest obstacle. The price. We can take it from there."

Zachary nodded, though Adele could tell he would have preferred to take her to the office, giving him more time to do the "sell."

Finally, he told her.

Adele's heart flipped. More than she had anticipated.

"That's the asking price," she pressed.

"Of course."

She clung to her purse, tapping her fingers on the strap as she did some quick mental calculations.

"If you could look at the financials, you'd have a much better idea of how this will easily pay for itself," Zachary continued.

"Easily" was a meaningless term to toss out when you were on the selling end of a business. She and Leah also needed to make a living wage.

"You're right," she agreed. "But I don't have time to check that out right now. Would you be willing to e-mail the financials to me?"

Zachary hesitated. Again, she knew he wanted to go over this in his own territory. "Sure," he said. "I think I can do that."

"Excellent. That way I can look them over on my own time."

Zachary handed her a business card and a pen. "Write your e-mail on this and I'll send them as soon as I'm back in the office."

Adele gave him a smile, scribbled her e-mail address on the card and handed it back. "Thanks so much for your time. This looks promising," she said, giving him the faint sliver of hope she knew he was looking for.

"It is. I have a few other people coming to have a look. I'm sure they'll agree with you."

Though Adele recognized his statement for the usual selling tactic it was, the thought gave her heart a little jolt of fear.

"I'm sure they would," she agreed, giving him a smile. "Thanks again. I'll be in touch once I see the numbers."

He shook her hand and escorted her out of the bakery. Thankfully the wind of the past few days was absent. The sun was shining, and the snow, piled up on the concrete planters along the street, glinted brightly.

"Thanks again, and hopefully I'll hear from you," Zachary said. Then he walked across the street to where his office was.

Adele took a look around the town. Brick buildings lined the street, two stories high. Wrought-iron lampposts marched along the brick sidewalk. Each business had a concrete planter in front of it. It was a pretty town. Some older buildings, a few newer ones. As she walked along the main street of the town, her eyes shifted upward to the ridge of mountains she glimpsed between the buildings. They weren't as close here as they were at the ranch, but they still created a compelling backdrop. Especially now, coated in snow, achingly white against a bluebird sky.

I could work here, Adele thought, pulling in a slow, steady breath. She could make a home here.

Are you sure? Do you dare? What if things don't work out with you and Wyatt?

Her mind ticked back over their time together. Yes, it was short. They hadn't been "together" for months.

But she felt a connection with him she had never felt with anyone else. A sense of rightness.

With that in mind, she stepped into her car and took a moment to send the pictures to Leah. As she started her car and waited for it to warm up, her phone binged.

Leah had sent a thumbs-up. Then added an enthusiastic text message.

This looks great. I love it. Love the location.

Adele lowered her phone, sending up a prayer of thanks. This was another affirmation. Another positive sign.

She drove to the grocery store with a light heart. Excited. She would phone Leah tonight, once she got the financials from Zachary. That would help her make a final decision.

She hurried through the grocery store, excited to see Wyatt and the kids. Excited to tell him what she had planned.

It took her only a few moments to get what they needed. She

knew her way around by now. But as she stopped to get bread, she shot a quick glance at the bakery section. Checking it out. *The competition*, she thought with a wry smile.

She felt a curious lift of her heart as she imagined the bakery she had just looked at. Imagined what she and Leah could do.

There was only one cashier open, so she got in line behind two other women. She checked her phone as another text message from Leah came through.

I'd like to come see for myself.

Adele grinned and replied. She slipped her phone into her pocket, smiling as the women ahead of her chatted with the cashier about the cold. Complained about the snow. The cashier was chatty and seemed to know them. Then the one turned to look back at the other.

And ice slipped through Adele's veins. Fear constricted her throat. She knew that face with its distinctively up-tilted blue eyes framed with long fake eyelashes. The prominent cheekbones.

Her hair was now gray streaked with blue instead of pink, but there was no mistaking this woman for anyone but Theresa. Wyatt's ex-wife.

"I want to head to Main Street after we're done here," Theresa said, flicking her hair back. "I want to stop at the bookstore and pick up something for the twins."

Maya and Maria. Theresa's daughters. And now the mother they had sobbed their little hearts out over was here. In Millar's Crossing.

Adele's heart raced as she remembered Wyatt's comment about Theresa's e-mail. How she wanted to have a relationship with the girls.

She blinked, spots dancing in front of her eyes. She forced herself to breathe, to calm herself.

This wasn't happening. Was it?

"Good idea. Though are you ready to see Wyatt again?" the other woman asked.

Theresa frowned, gave a shrug, then glanced at her cell phone as it sent out a flurry of bells. "I should take this. I'll meet you outside."

The other woman nodded, pushing her groceries farther down the belt toward the cashier.

Adele watched Theresa walk away, her slim figure encased in snug blue jeans, a puffy down jacket. She looked exotic and beautiful.

"I can't believe Theresa is here," the cashier said to the woman in line, slowly scanning her items, not seeming to be in a rush. "I never thought she'd come back to Millar's Crossing."

"Well, people change. She's changed," the woman answered. "I think she'd love to reconnect with Wyatt. I keep telling her she'll be sorry if she doesn't give it another try with him. Besides, she's got those adorable twins."

"I heard Wyatt was seeing someone else."

Adele clung to her grocery cart, looking down. Hoping that Miss Chatty Cashier didn't recognize her.

"Well, I know Wyatt has always had a thing for Theresa, and I think kids need to be with their mom."

"I agree. I hope it all works out," the cashier said.

Adele swallowed, her throat dry. She looked down at the few groceries she had bought. The bread, milk, eggs, juice for the twins, a bag of their favorite chips. Some licorice for Dean.

Theresa was back. She wanted to reconnect with Wyatt. With the kids.

Unwelcome tears pooled in her eyes. Sorrow thickened her throat. She had to leave.

She spun around and strode away, ignoring the cashier calling out after her.

As she walked out she saw Theresa off to one side of the doorway, chatting on her cell phone, laughing.

The sound was like an arrow to her heart. Then Theresa looked up at her, frowning as Adele found she couldn't look away. She wasn't sure how she managed, but she lifted her head and walked over as Theresa lowered her cell phone. "Can I help you?" Theresa asked.

"You don't know me, but I feel I should tell you that Wyatt has a little boy in his house now. His name is Dean, and he's Wyatt's son." Her voice faltered as Theresa frowned, looking puzzled but interested. "I really hope...I want you...please take good care of him when you get back together with Wyatt. He's a good kid."

Then, before Theresa could say anything more, Adele scurried back to her car.

Her legs felt like rubber and she couldn't see past the tears now spilling out of her eyes. A sudden tightness pinched her forehead, swelling through her brain.

Theresa was back. The girls' mother had returned.

Adele got into her car, laid her head on the steering wheel, stunned, struggling with this new information. She blew out a breath, wondering what had gotten into her just a moment ago. Why she had even gone to talk to her.

It was for Dean, she told herself. She had to make sure Dean would be okay.

Theresa had to know about Dean.

And if she was reconciling with Wyatt, Adele knew she had to get out of the way.

Families need to be together.

She abandoned her children.

The woman said she had changed. And she had come back, like she had said to Wyatt.

What would Adele do now? How could she meet Wyatt in town, now that she found out Theresa wanted to come back?

Did it matter? He didn't seem to miss Theresa. Had never spoken positively about her.

And yet...

Theresa was back. She was buying a gift for her children. Her daughters. Adele thought of the twins. How sad they said they were that they missed her.

Adele remembered her own childhood, wondering about her own biological mother. Wondering what her life would have been like had she lived. She remembered crying about her even though she'd been so young when her mother passed away.

Kids need their mom.

Family needs family.

Adele knew she couldn't meet Wyatt now. Knew she couldn't carry this on any further with Theresa in town. But he was waiting for her and she needed to let him know.

Her fingers hovered over the screen, wondering what to say. *Sorry?*

I care about you?

I love you?

Those last words slipped so easily into her mind. But they almost choked her.

Because she knew it was true.

She shook her emotions off, fought down the pain and sorrow. Everything had changed now. Her world had spun on its axis and she had to release her own needs and expectations.

Should she lie? Tell him she had to meet with Leah?

No. She couldn't do that. *Keep it simple*, she told herself.

She put together a quick text, keeping her language vague. Her hand hovered over the Send button, then, shaking off her second thoughts she hit it then turned her phone off. She didn't want to hear anything back from him.

Didn't want to know what was going on.

She wasn't ready to go back to the Airbnb. She wasn't ready to face anyone yet.

She drove out of the parking lot and headed north. Down

the same road she and Dean had traveled that very first day. A day that seemed like eons ago.

"Where is Adele?" Maya asked as Wyatt buckled her in her car seat.

"I don't know." Wyatt still wasn't sure what to make of the terse text she sent him canceling lunch. He supposed she got busy. But with what?

His confusion was tinged with concern. Things were still so new between them. Was she having second thoughts?

The thought sent a chill down his spine. She had seemed a bit off when he left her this morning. As if she had things on her mind.

He got Maria and Maya in their seats, made sure Dean was buckled up, then got in the truck. He pulled the keys out of his pocket and started the truck but then sat, staring sightlessly out the front window. Something had happened. He knew it.

He pulled his phone out and texted her again, hit Send, and watched the screen. But nothing. He gave it a few more moments, but no dots bounced across the bottom of the screen.

Why wasn't she replying?

He pulled out of the parking lot and turned, heading for home.

"I hope Adele isn't hungry," Dean said. "She didn't come and have lunch with us."

Wyatt glanced in the rearview mirror and gave him what he hoped was a reassuring smile. "I'm sure she'll be okay. Maybe she got something to eat somewhere else."

As he drove through town, he gave in to an impulse and turned toward the Airbnb that Adele was staying at.

Her car wasn't there.

"Just stay here, kids. I need to go talk to Mrs. Flikkema. He turned the truck off and strode up the snow-covered walk.

He knocked on the door, shoving his hands in his pockets, looking around. As if hoping Adele might suddenly appear.

"Well, Wyatt, how nice to see you," Mrs. Flikkema said, her smile brightening her face.

"I'm looking for Adele. Do you know if she's here?" he asked.

Mrs. Flikkema looked past him, then shook her head. "I don't see her car here. I know she was here last night and then left early this morning. But I don't think she's been here since. I try not to be too nosy about my guests."

Wyatt nodded, thinking. Wondering where else Adele could be.

"If you see her, can you tell her I need to talk to her?"

"Of course. I'll pass that on."

"Thanks." Wyatt turned and jogged down the steps toward the truck. He got in, fighting down his frustration.

Had Adele changed her mind about them?

The question slithered through his gut. He didn't want to think about it. Didn't want to contemplate it.

Then why wasn't she answering her phone?

"Did you find Adele?" Dean asked.

Wyatt heard the worry in his voice and reminded himself that Adele wouldn't leave without at least saying good-bye to Dean. So that was out of the question.

He fought down his worry as he drove back to the ranch.

When he got there, he saw a car parked by the ranch house. Relief flowed through him, but as he got closer, he realized it wasn't Adele's car. It belonged to the nanny.

With a sinking heart, he parked the truck and turned it off. As he got out, he forced a smile to his face. The kids didn't need to know his concern.

"Nanny is here," Maya called out, pointing past Wyatt. As he set his daughter on the ground, Wyatt glanced back in time to see Ruby coming down the steps.

Maya ran toward her, arms wide, as if greeting a long-lost friend.

Ruby swept her up in a big hug, then walked over to Maria, who was also running toward her.

It was a happy reunion, and any other time Wyatt would have been thrilled to see her again.

Just not right now.

Dean got out of the truck, looking uncertain.

"We have a new friend," Maya said, dragging Ruby toward Dean. "His name is Dean. And he is living with us."

Ruby shot Wyatt a puzzled look.

"I'll explain it to you later," he said.

"Well then, it's lovely to meet you, Dean," Ruby said, holding her hand out to him.

Dean glanced at Wyatt as if to make sure it was okay.

Wyatt crouched down in front of him, placing a comforting hand on his shoulder.

"Nanny sometimes comes and takes care of the twins for me, so now she'll be taking care of you too sometimes."

"What about Adele?"

And wasn't that the question of the afternoon?

"I'm sure Adele will let us know soon what's happening." It was all he could give the little guy.

Together they walked up to the house. Before they stepped inside, Wyatt shot one more look over his shoulder, as if hoping by some small miracle Adele would show up.

And on the heels of that came another horrible thought. What if something happened to her?

He stepped into the house and his phone pinged.

He glanced at the screen and relief trickled through him. It was Adele.

Sorry I couldn't make it to the restaurant. Got things on my mind. Will text you more later.

And that was it.

Wyatt wanted to throw his phone across the porch, but he kept everything inside while he helped Ruby undress the kids.

"Do you mind watching the kids until suppertime?" Wyatt asked Ruby. "I need to do some office work."

He had nothing of the sort to do, but he needed some time alone.

CHAPTER FIFTEEN

"I'm sorry if I raised your hopes, but I don't think this is happening." Adele sat in her car, parked in a pullout off the highway. After she had left town, she had driven around for a couple hours. Thinking. Grieving.

Now she was talking to her partner.

"Explain this to me again?" Leah asked.

Adele rubbed her fingers across her forehead, wishing she could ease away the headache that had taken residence there.

"Wyatt's ex-wife is back. It's as simple as that. She wants to reconcile with Wyatt, and I have to get out of the way. Those girls need their mother and I need to give that family a chance, for the girls' sake. And in order for that to happen, I have to leave."

"Have you talked to Wyatt about this?"

"What am I supposed to say? I'm happy for you that your wife is back?"

"Or you could just find out if that's what's happening?"

Adele sighed. "I heard it myself. His wife bought a present

CAROLYNE AARSEN

for the girls, and she's taking it to the ranch. Her friend told the cashier who, apparently, they know quite well, that Theresa and Wyatt are getting back together again. Pretty straightforward as far as I'm concerned."

Leah's silence reinforced her concerns.

"And what about Dean?"

What about him indeed?

Her heart twisted at the thought of how she would explain to Dean what was going on. For a few bright and shining moments she had seen herself as his mother, as Wyatt's wife. Even though he hadn't asked her, she knew Wyatt was a responsible person. He wouldn't do anything to jeopardize his little daughters' emotions by bringing someone into their life if he wasn't serious.

She wondered how Theresa would be with him.

She slammed her mind down on those thoughts. She couldn't go any further than the next few moments.

"The financials on that bakery looked good," Leah said. "And the price is high, but I'm sure we can swing payments and wages based on the income. Are you sure you don't want to go ahead with it anyway?"

Adele held that thought, then shook it off. Did she want to be around Wyatt and see him with his wife?

Did she want to see Dean with her?

"I don't. But we still have time to hit the auction in Edmonton. I can meet you there this afternoon."

"Okay, I guess that's what we'll do then. You'll have to rush. The first items are going on the block at five o'clock."

Adele glanced at the clock on the dash. No time to go back to the Airbnb to get her stuff. She could grab a change of clothes at a mall. "Did you rent a hotel?"

"I did."

"Do you mind if I bunk up with you tonight?"

"Of course not. I'll see you later."

Adele said good-bye, then held the phone a little longer, knowing she had one more job to do. She pulled in a hard breath and sent a text to Wyatt, asking him to tell Dean she would be gone tonight but would be back soon. She hit send, then turned her phone off, turned around and headed north. When all this was done, she would come back to Millar's Crossing and say good-bye to Dean properly.

Hopefully without Wyatt around.

Wyatt stared at the book on his lap he'd been trying to read for the past hour, but none of the words made any sense.

It was nine o'clock. The kids had been sleeping for the past two hours.

Ruby had made supper for them and then left, promising to come again tomorrow.

Adele's last text still rang through his head raising more questions and creating more anger. All she had said was to please tell Dean she needed to go to a sale. That she would be back in a day or so. No personal message for him.

Dean had been stoic when Wyatt had passed the message on, but he could tell that the little guy was concerned.

Anger flashed through Wyatt. It was one thing for Adele to leave him, but to leave Dean like this?

She had sent him another text telling him she was in Edmonton at the auction.

Of course. Her dream.

Is that why she'd abandoned them? Was that what she had on her mind?

Wyatt laid his head back against the couch, closing his eyes. He had tried to pray, but wasn't sure what to pray for. He thought he knew Adele, thought they had something going. He'd been daring to make some plans for the future.

And now?

A hard knock on the door broke into his questions.

Again his heart did that stupid jump of hope. He pushed it down, got up, and walked to the door wondering who else would come this time of night.

He opened the door and his heart twisted and clenched in his chest.

"Hey there, Wyatt," Theresa said, wavering as she stood in front of him, illuminated by the lights of the car parked behind her. She held out a plastic bag. "I bought this for the girls."

Wyatt stared at her, trying to figure out what was going on. "What are you doing here?"

"I told you. I brought my little girls a present. A good-bye present."

Her words were slurred, and her eyes glassy.

She'd been drinking.

Wyatt took the bag from her, still confused, old anger rising against her. Anger not only at her, but at himself. Theresa was a solid reminder of his taste in women. Obviously he couldn't find one who understood commitment.

But even as all this went through his head, he latched on to the last thing she had said.

"What you mean, a good-bye present?"

She gave him a goofy grin just as the door of the car opened and another woman came up and onto the porch. Wyatt had to squint against the bright lights to figure out who it was. Then as she came into view, he shook his head. He should have known. Theresa's buddy in crime.

"Hey, Laura. Should've figured you'd be here too."

"Designated driver," she said with a shrug. She turned to Theresa. "We gotta get going, girl, if you want to make your flight."

"Stupid red-eye," Theresa grumbled. "Don't know why I can't fly to Australia at a more reasonable time."

"Australia?"

"Yep. Got a job there." She turned to Laura and grabbed her arm. "Laura said I should try to get together with you again. But I told her there was no way. Not doing that again. Don't like kids."

That much was obvious, Wyatt wanted to say. But he kept his thoughts to himself.

Wyatt was growing colder, but there was no way he was inviting Theresa and Laura into the house. Especially with the kids in the house and Theresa in this condition.

"Speaking of kids. What's with this Dean kid?" Theresa asked, frowning.

"What you know about Dean?"

"Some chick at the grocery store comes up to me. Says something about how you got a kid called Dean. That I gotta take good care of him. Like that's gonna happen."

This was growing more bizarre every moment.

"Did you know her?" Wyatt asked, puzzled.

"Never saw her before in my life."

Wyatt frowned, then remembered Adele said she had to go to the grocery store. "Was she tall, slender, wavy brown hair and freckles?"

Theresa gave him a sly grin. "New girlfriend?"

Wyatt didn't honor her question with a response.

"Yeah. That's what she looked like," Theresa said. "Wearing some kind of blue puffy vest under a winter coat. Jeans and cowboy boots of all things. Walking Millar's Crossing cliché."

That was Adele, all right. Except for the negative cliché part.

Wyatt struggled to put everything together, wondering why Adele had talked to Theresa. "How did she know who you were?"

"Gabby mouth here was chatting at Nancy, the cashier. Girl we went to school with." Theresa fluttered a hand at Laura. "I think I saw that chick standing behind Laura. Next thing I know she walks up to me telling me about this Dean kid. Told me to take care of him when I get back together with you."

And then everything fell into place.

"She thought we were getting back together? How?" Wyatt looked at Theresa. "You can't possibly think—"

"Don't worry. Ain't happening. Don't know where she got that idea."

Laura laughed then. "Sorry, I think she must've heard me talking to the cashier. I said a bunch of stuff about how I hoped that Theresa would give you another chance. I mean, you're a great guy, and I think she's making a mistake. Anyhow, that woman must have overheard me say that. But I don't know why she should care."

"That was weird," Theresa agreed. "But you know I'm not coming back."

The words hung in the air, then with a deep sigh, Laura tugged on Theresa's arm. "Look, sweetie, if you're not getting together with this guy, we really gotta get going."

"That's right. You and me and Australia, baby," Theresa said, waving a hand in the air. "Say hi to the little girls. Actually, say good-bye. Don't think I'll be coming back."

Then she grew serious, her eyes holding his, growing sorrowful.

"I'm sorry, Wyatt. Sorry I couldn't be what you wanted me to be. I'm just not that person."

To Wyatt's dismay her voice grew shaky, and she sniffed. She looked like she was about to cry. Then she blinked and shook it off. "Sorry again. Sorry for no big reunion, just a good-bye."

Without another word, she turned, stumbled, then righted herself and walked over to the car.

Laura turned to Wyatt. "I'm sorry too. I shouldn't have brought her here. I guess I was kind of hoping...and she was doing the drunk-crying thing about how she should never have treated you so bad...I just thought...but I guess I was wrong."

Then with another shrug, she turned and left.

Wyatt watched as the car reversed, turned, and then headed down the driveway. A wink of the taillights and then they were gone.

He shivered, closing the door, leaning against it a moment. He wasn't sure what had just happened.

He looked down at the bag and opened it. He saw the books inside then shook his head. He wasn't sure if he would tell the girls about Theresa's visit right away or not. That would have to wait for another time.

For now, it looked like Theresa would be on the other side of the world. Far removed from them.

He had a text to send.

CHAPTER SIXTEEN

"So what do we do?"

Leah sat beside Adele in the heated auction building, both huddled over a cup of hot chocolate. In the background they heard the yodeling of the auctioneer, selling yet another item. People milled about them, carrying bid numbers, talking on cell phones. All filled with purpose.

Adele stirred her hot chocolate, still unable to take a sip. From the looks of her still-full cup, neither could Leah. This morning neither had eaten breakfast, and Adele knew she needed to put something in her stomach.

"I don't know. Still trying to absorb this. Don't know how else to say this other than it sucks."

Ten minutes ago, the equipment they had so hoped to purchase had gone for half again as much over the amount they were prepared to bid. Two other people besides them were interested, which was all it took to send the prices rocketing upward. The lot that had sold last night had also gone higher, but that wasn't necessary equipment. Nothing they couldn't buy wholesale elsewhere. But the ovens, cooling racks, heavy-duty mixers, and tools that had been on the block this morning were the main event as far as they were concerned.

And she and Leah had been outbid on them. By more than they could afford.

"I truly didn't think it would go that high," Adele said, easing out a deep sigh. "I did my research. Checked prices."

Leah laid a gentle hand on hers. "I know you did. Don't beat yourself up. It's not your fault these people caught auction fever. Better them than us."

Adele gave her a feeble smile of thanks. "You're right. But it still hurts."

"I know I'm right. And yeah, it still hurts. Though I wonder if we can't check—" she stopped short, waving her hand between them as if to erase any words she might say.

Adele guessed she would have mentioned the bakery in Millar's Crossing.

"Sorry. I know where you were going. I can't go to Millar's Crossing. If Theresa is trying to make a go with Wyatt, I have to keep my distance. It's not fair to Wyatt or Dean." Besides, there was no way she could live in Millar's Crossing and risk running into the reunited family from time to time. Which, she was sure, would happen. It would be heartrendingly difficult.

"I know. You're right. I guess I was just trying to keep the dream alive."

Adele attempted another sip, her mind spinning between her broken dreams and Wyatt, Dean and the girls.

All the way to Edmonton they had been on her mind. She had to fight the urge to text Wyatt. To explain. But she had to keep her distance. So she'd turned her phone off. Then, as if to add insult to injury, it had dropped out of the car when she got out at the hotel, right into a puddle of melted snow. She'd had no way of drying it out and now it didn't work.

Just as well.

"I hate to be pushy, but what's next?"

"I should get back to Millar's Crossing and get my stuff. If my laptop wasn't there, I'm sure I would just leave the clothes behind."

"Do you want me to come along? For moral support?"

Adele shook her head. "Thanks a lot, but you need to get back to Whitehorse. No sense in adding to your trip."

"I don't like the idea of you traveling with a non-working cell phone."

"People have done it for years," Adele said with a light chuckle.

"Yeah, but there were pay phones then."

"I'll be fine," Adele assured her. "The roads are dry and the forecast looks good. It's just time and miles. I can listen to the radio for a change instead of baking podcasts."

They sat in silence for another few moments, then Adele glanced at the large clock above the cashier at the far end of the building. "I should go. I'll see you when I see you," she said. "If I get a hotel tonight, I'll give you a dingle."

"Sounds good." They said a quick good-bye, then went their separate ways.

All the way back to Millar's Crossing, driving down the road she had driven all those weeks ago, Adele struggled to listen to the radio and keep her mind off Wyatt and Dean and the girls. Each song reminded her of what she had lost.

For the first time in a long while hope had been part of her vocabulary. Had been a ray of light in her life.

At least Wyatt and Dean were reunited. Father and son.

Now, mother and daughters.

She hoped, prayed, that Theresa would be kind to Dean. Would take him in.

She struggled with the image she'd had of the woman. Tried not to judge her from the brief encounter she'd had and from what Wyatt had told her.

Please take care of them all, she prayed as the miles rolled past and the mountains drew nearer.

Finally, after long hours, she pulled into Millar's Crossing. It was still early afternoon. Time enough to get her stuff and then leave. Put as many miles between her and the memories as possible.

She parked in front of Mrs. Flikkema's place, memories assaulting her. For a few precious, beautiful days, she'd had a dream. She'd had the possibility of a life and a future with an amazing man.

She clutched her chest as a sharp pain, almost like a heart attack, radiated through her chest.

No Wyatt. No Dean.

No bakery dreams.

She tried not to look too far ahead. Once again, she was back to where she had been each time she ended up back at her father's house. Not daring to think what might happen. How she would cope.

One minute, one hour at a time. Don't think too far ahead.

But even as all the losses in her life seemed to pile up, she thought of the one thing that had changed. Her openness to God's love. Her acceptance of the peace He offered her.

Something she knew could never be taken away from her. It had been a hard journey, and she knew she would have times of heartache and regret, but one thing she had learned was that God was always faithful. It had just taken a few twists and turns to get there.

She pressed cool fingers to her aching head, sending up yet another prayer for peace. For patience. For wisdom to know what to do.

And she released Wyatt, Dean, and the girls to God's care.

As she did, she felt a blanket of comfort surround her. She didn't have to be the one taking care of them.

God would watch over them.

Pulling in another breath, she got out of the car. She hadn't been able to call ahead, but she assumed that Mrs. Flikkema hadn't changed the entry code. She punched it in, heard the lock disengage, and stepped inside. At least it was warm.

She walked to the kitchen cupboard, wondering if she had any rice she could put her phone in. She'd read somewhere that doing so would help dry it out. But nothing. There were only a few groceries in the cupboard and nothing in the fridge. When she had come back here, she hadn't figured on eating here, so she hadn't restocked.

It didn't take much to get her clothes packed up. Her toiletries from the bathroom. She slipped her laptop with all its plans and dreams into her backpack and choked down a sob.

No. She was doing this. She was moving on.

Please help me, Lord, to trust in You, she prayed.

She pulled in a deep breath, walked around the suite one more time, and then slung her purse and her backpack over her shoulder. Grabbing her suitcase, she headed to the door.

Someone was knocking on it. Hard.

She looked different, Wyatt thought. An anxiousness that usually surrounded her seemed to have faded away.

She looked peaceful.

"Hey there," she said, her voice quiet. She blinked, then looked away.

Wyatt glanced down at her suitcase, the backpack and laptop bag slung over her shoulder. "You're leaving?"

"Yes. Back to Whitehorse." She made a move, like she wanted to go past him, but he shifted, stopping her.

"Do you want to go back?"

She bit her lip, still avoiding his gaze. Then she released a harsh breath. "What do you want, Wyatt?"

He was taken aback at her tone, then realized how this must look to her.

He wanted to explain everything, but not on a doorstep of someone else's house with the wind swirling snow around them.

"Theresa is gone. She's not at the ranch. She's moving to Australia." He felt he needed to at least say that.

She shot him a shocked look. "What?"

"Please, I'm freezing. Can we go somewhere warmer? Where I can get a cup of coffee and we can find a quiet corner to talk?"

She hesitated, then nodded. "I'll follow you."

He had hoped she would come with him in the truck, but this might be for the best.

"There's a place on Main Street," he said. "Not far from the bakery. It's called Coffee on the Corner."

Another nod.

"Can I help you with that?" he asked, pointing to her suitcase.

"I'm fine."

She didn't sound fine, which made him wonder if Theresa was the problem or if she was having second thoughts.

He couldn't go there. Not now. He had prayed all the way here, and he had to believe that somehow, once they talked...

He had to believe that what had happened between them was real. Had to believe that he could trust his own emotions in this.

The coffee shop held only a few people this time of day, and he found a spot tucked in the back.

"What do you want?" he asked as Adele settled in at the table.

She still wasn't looking at him, which concerned him deeply. But she was here, so that was a plus.

"Just coffee. Black."

"She's got lattes and all kinds of other stuff," Wyatt offered. "Cookies? Banana bread?"

Adele shook her head but then gave him a gentle smile,

easing the tension that had been holding his shoulders since he left the ranch. "Just coffee, please. Black."

He made quick work of his order. Janie, the owner of the coffee shop, asked about the girls, and he gave a non-committal reply. He could see that she was curious about Adele, but he didn't give her any more information than he had to.

He brought the coffees back and sat. But now that he and Adele were alone, his mind went blank. He took a few sips of his coffee, trying to think of what to say.

"You said Theresa isn't around?" Adele finally asked, breaking the tense silence between them.

"Yes. Apparently she and her friend Laura, the woman she was with, are moving to Australia." Wyatt latched onto her question, relieved that she was willing to talk about what happened. "She came to Millar's Crossing to say good-bye, though she didn't want to see the girls."

"That's strange."

"That's Theresa. Strange is her middle name. Along with unfaithful and uncommitted." He couldn't stop the bitter tone that crept into his voice. "I still can't believe she didn't even want to see her own daughters."

"I understand, but maybe it's for the better. Seeing her would just confuse and hurt them." Adele's quiet comment eased his anger.

"You're right. As always." He smiled over at her, frustrated with the awkwardness that had risen between them. This wasn't how he had envisioned this meeting going. Their eyes held, and he wished he could find the right words to express himself.

Could use a little help here, Lord, he prayed.

Then she smiled again, and he took a chance, reaching across the table to catch her hand. Her fingers twined around his and the awkwardness slipped away.

"I'm sorry that you thought Theresa was coming back. That

you had to go through that. You need to know I feel nothing for her. That she doesn't matter to me."

"Don't apologize for something you had no control over. I just..." She paused, looking down at their entwined hands, her fingers stroking his. Then she looked up at him, her eyes bright. "I just didn't want to get in the way. If you were reuniting with her. For the kids' sake and, well, for yours. Family has to stay together."

Wyatt felt a nudge of sorrow at her last words. An echo of her own life and her own desires. "I agree, but Theresa doesn't have the same notion of family that you have. I know how important family is to you. But I also know how important you are to me." He drew in a long, steadying breath, taking another chance. "I don't want you to leave. I want you to stay. I know you had a dream of building a bakery, and I'm hoping you might do that here. In Millar's Crossing. I want us to spend proper time together. Get to know each other better. I know that we have something wonderful, and I know that it's worth investing in." He shook his head, looking down. "And didn't that last comment sound romantic."

But she was chuckling, her hands tightening on his, her other hand covering them both. "I agree. And I want to spend more time with you and the kids as well. I care about you. A lot." Then she released a light laugh. "In fact, I...I love you."

Wyatt's eyes flew up at that, surprise and joy flooding him. He stared at her, realizing what this statement cost her. "Oh, my dear girl," he said, unable to keep his distance. He pulled her closer, leaned in, and kissed her. Hard. Then he pulled back. "I love you too. So much that I don't think the words do it justice."

They sat a moment, letting the words spin around them, filling the emptiness in their souls. Wyatt thought he would never stop smiling.

"Can we go back to the ranch?" he asked, his hands holding hers. Tight. "I want us to be all together. Again."

"That's all I want too," she said. Then she leaned forward and kissed him.

He pulled her to her feet, coffees forgotten. She grabbed her purse and then, hand in hand, not caring who saw, they walked out of the coffee shop.

CHAPTER SEVENTEEN

"*A*re we giving the surprise here?" Maya asked from the back of the truck. "I want to do it right away."

"We will. Be patient." Wyatt gave her a quick grin, then angle-parked his truck beside another truck that had the name of a construction company on the side.

Adele and Leah had been busy the past few weeks doing some necessary renovations on the bakery they had purchased over a month ago.

It had taken a bit of time to finagle all the financing but when it went through, they'd had an impromptu party in the old bakery. The next day, they went to work. But it had been hard to find a finishing carpenter in town so they'd had to hire Connor from Rockyview, an hour's drive away.

"Will Miss Adele like the present?" Maria asked.

"It comes from Dad. Of course she'll like it," Dean said, helping the girls unbuckle from their car seat.

It had only been the past couple of weeks that Dean, under

encouragement from Adele, had started calling Wyatt, Dad. It still caught him unawares and it still created a gentle warmth.

"Okay, kiddos, let's do this." Wyatt was surprised at how nervous he was. He'd chosen a time when he knew Leah was gone and Adele would be alone. He had phoned ten minutes out of town and found out that Connor was having lunch at Coffee on the Corner. Otherwise he would have had to figure something else out.

He had hoped to do this properly. All romantic and stuff, but Reuben was moving into the house next week and the weather was still chilly even though yesterday's chinook was a promise of spring coming.

And the kids knew he had a present for Adele and were getting antsy.

He patted his pocket to make sure the small box was still there. Dean held the other boxes in the bag he carried, proud of his part in this surprise.

"Okay, we have to be quiet and keep this a secret until I say," Wyatt said, putting his finger to his lips in warning.

Maya and Maria nodded, looking solemn. They had practiced their parts and were anxious to see this through.

Wyatt took a deep breath, sent up a prayer for courage, pulled open the new door of the bakery, and let the girls and Dean go in. He followed right behind.

The first thing he noticed was the smell of fresh-cut wood blended with paint. The display cases in the front had been installed. The glass gleamed under the bright overhead lights. Shelves lined the one wall, stained a dark brown, a contrast to the soft green of the walls. Adele and Leah had spent hours trying to decide on the color. Wyatt had kept out of that discussion, unable to see the differences between the four shades of green they were choosing between.

But it looked warm and inviting.

"Don't touch the cases," Wyatt warned as Maya and Maria pulled faces at themselves in the glass. Dean was headed to the back where Wyatt could hear a radio playing in the background, Adele humming along.

The girls finally noticed and charged to the back of the bakery, calling out Adele's name.

"Remember, it's a surprise," Dean called out, catching up to them.

Wyatt followed, laughing at the kids' exuberance.

Adele stood on a ladder against the back wall of the bakery, paintbrush in hand, bandanna protecting her hair. She turned as the kids called out her name.

"Well, hey there. This is a nice surprise." She set the paintbrush down, wiped her hands on a rag, and then descended the ladder. She shot Wyatt a special smile that could still make his knees feel wobbly.

Each day they spent together only reinforced what he wanted to do right here, right now.

She walked over to Wyatt, and he pulled her close in a tight hug, then brushed a kiss over her lips.

"We have a surprise, a big surprise," the girls called out, dancing around the large butcher block table in the center of the back room.

"Really, this sounds intriguing," Adele said.

"Wyatt-Dad has to go first," Dean said, frowning a warning at the girls.

Adele smiled at Dean's stumble. A rare one for him once he made the move.

"What's going on?" Adele asked, turning to Wyatt, her hand still resting on his chest.

Wyatt sucked in a deep breath, wishing once again he could have chosen a more romantic locale. But once the kids were in on the secret, he knew he had only days to pull this off.

So he gave her a bright smile, pulled in a calming breath. Then he dug into his pocket and drew out the small velvet box. Another breath, another prayer and he knelt on the sawdust sprinkled floor, held out the box, and looked up at her. "Adele Marten, love of my life and blessing to our kids. Will you marry me?"

Adele's hands had flown to her mouth, her eyes shining with unshed tears as Wyatt spoke. Then, to his surprise, she dropped to the floor in front of him and hugged him tight, pressing her head into his neck.

"Of course I will. Of course."

"Is she crying?" Wyatt heard Maria whisper, a tinge of worry in her voice.

"Yes, I am," Adele said, her voice muffled. Then she drew back, swiped at her face, and gave Wyatt, and the kids now gathered behind him a brilliant smile. "But it's a happy cry."

"Oh. That's good, right?" Maria asked.

"Very good," Adele assured her.

Wyatt pulled the ring out of the box. He took Adele's hand and slipped the diamond solitaire onto her paint-smeared fingers. Thankfully, it was the right size.

"Oh, look," she said, pushing it all the way down her finger and holding it up. "Look how beautiful."

"We have something too," Dean announced, stepping forward, one hand holding his bag, the other urging the girls to join him.

"I give, I want to give it," Maya called out.

Wyatt stopped Maya from reaching out to the bag Dean held. The boy was so easygoing and so easily pushed around by Maya that Wyatt needed to intervene from time to time.

"No. Dean is giving it."

Maya looked like she was about to pull out a pout, but then Dean was giving Adele the bag.

"There's presents in there. From the three of us," he said, coming up beside her as she took it from him.

Adele bit her lip, shooting Wyatt a questioning look. He just grinned at her.

She took another jeweler's box out of the bag. A long, narrow one. She carefully opened it. "A charm bracelet," she said. "It's beautiful."

"It's from all of us," Maya said, unable to contain herself a second longer, surging forward, pushing past Wyatt. "See the ornaments? That one is from me." She pointed to the princess one. Then Maria joined them. "I gave you the cupcake one. 'Cause I love cupcakes."

"And this one is from me," Dean said, pointing to the family tree charm he had chosen. "Because you always say family is important, and we're going to be a family. And this one is from Dad." He pointed to the heart charm.

Adele's eyes shimmered again as her eyes shifted over each of the children.

"What a perfect gift. I love it so much. I'll always think of each of you when I wear it."

"And there's room for more," Dean said, nodding, grinning up at her.

"I see that." She pulled it out of the box and Wyatt joined her to help her put it on. He clicked the clasp, then she held up her wrist. "So pretty."

Her ring sparkled as brightly as her eyes.

Wyatt moved closer, pulled her into his arms, and gave her another hug, another kiss.

"Group hug," Maya called out, slipping between them. Maria joined her and then Dean was pulled into the circle.

The circle of love. The circle of family.

"I don't think my heart could be fuller," Adele said, her arms embracing the girls and Dean, her hands resting on Wyatt's.

"Mine either," Wyatt returned.

"We're a family, a family," Maya called out, wiggling her pleasure.

"That we are," Wyatt said. "That we are," he repeated, looking around the group. His family.

Their family.

OTHER SERIES

I have many other books for you to enjoy. Check them out here.

FAMILY BONDS

#1 SEEKING HOME

A rancher who suffered a tragic loss. A single mother on the edge. Can these two find the courage to face a romantic new beginning?

#2 CHOOSING HOME

If you like emergency room drama, second chances, and quaint small-town settings, then you'll adore this romance.

#3 COMING HOME

He thought she chose a hotel over him. She thought he loved money more than her. Years later, can they fill the emptiness in their hearts?

#4 FINDING HOME

She's hiding a terrible truth. He's trying to overcome his scandalous history. Together, forgiveness might give them a second chance.

FAMILY TIES

Four siblings trying to finding their way back to family and faith

A COWBOY'S REUNION

He's still reeling from the breakup. She's ashamed of what she did. Can a chance reunion mend the fence, or are some hearts forever broken? If you like second chance stories, buried passions, and big country settings, then you'll love this emotional novel.

"I enjoyed this book and had trouble putting it down and had to finish it. If the rest of this series is this great, I look forward to reading more books by Carolyne Aarsen." Karen Semones - Amazon Review

THE COWBOY'S FAMILY

She's desperate. He's loyal. Will a dark lie hold them back from finding love on the ranch? If you like determined heroines, charming cowboys, and family dramas, then you'll love this heartfelt novel.

"What a wonderful series! The first book is Cowboy's Reunion. Tricia's story begins in that book. Emotional stories with wonderful characters. Looking forward to the rest of the books in this series." Jutzie - Amazon reviewer

TAMING THE COWBOY

A saddle bronc trying to prove himself worthy to a father who never loved him. A wedding planner whose ex-fiancee was too busy chasing his own dreams to think of hers. Two people, completely wrong for each other who yet need each other in ways they never realized. Can they let go of their own plans to find a way to heal together?

"This is the third book in the series and I have loved them all. . . . can't wait to see what happens with the last sibling." - Amazon reviewer

THE COWBOY'S RETURN

The final book in the Family Ties Series:

He enlisted in the military, leaving his one true love behind.

She gave herself to a lesser man and paid a terrible price.

In their hometown of Rockyview, they can choose to come together or say a final goodbye...

'This author did an amazing job of turning heartache into happiness with realism and inspirational feeling." Marlene - Amazon Reviewer

SWEETHEARTS OF SWEET CREEK

Come back to faith and love

#1 HOMECOMING

Be swept away by this sweet romance of a woman's search for belonging and second chances and the rugged rancher who helps her heal.

#2 - HER HEARTS PROMISE

When the man she once loved reveals a hidden truth about the past, Nadine has to choose between justice and love.

#3 - CLOSE TO HIS HEART

Can love triumph over tragedy?

#4 - DIVIDED HEARTS

To embrace a second chance at love, they'll need to discover the truths of the past and the possibilities of the future…

#5 - A HERO AT HEART

If you like rekindled chemistry, family drama, and small, beautiful towns, then you'll love this story of heart and heroism.

#6 - A MOTHER'S HEART

If you like matchmaking daughters, heartfelt stories of mending broken homes, and fixer-upper romance, then this story of second chances is just right for you.

HOLMES CROSSING SERIES

The Only Best Place is the first book in the Holmes Crossing Series.

#1 THE ONLY BEST PLACE

One mistake jeopardized their relationship. Will surrendering her dreams to save their marriage destroy her?

#2 ALL IN ONE PLACE

She has sass, spunk and a haunting secret.

#3 THIS PLACE

Her secret could destroy their second chance at love

#4 A SILENCE IN THE HEART

Can a little boy, an injured kitten and a concerned vet with his own past pain, break down the walls of Tracy's heart?

#5 ANY MAN OF MINE

Living with three brothers has made Danielle tired of guys and cowboys. She wants a man. But is she making the right choice?

#6 A PLACE IN HER HEART

Her new boss shattered her dreams and now she has to work with him. But his vision for the magazine she loves puts them at odds. Can they find a way to work together or will his past bitterness blind him to future love.

Made in United States
North Haven, CT
21 January 2022

15055710R00133